MW01717217

THE CROWN AND THE CLOAK

BY

G.H. BABAGILO

Babagilo
A JOURNEY IN INK

The Crown and The Cloak

G.H. BABAGILO

Copyright © 2020 by Guy Hazan

All Rights Reserved

This book is a work of fiction. Names, characters, business organizations, places, events and incidents are the products of the author's imagination or are used fictitiously. The author's use of names of actual persons (living or dead), places, and characters is incidental to the purposes of the plot, and is not intended to change the entirely fictional character of the work or to disparage any company or its products or services.

No part of this book may be used or reproduced in any manner whatsoever without written permission except in the case of brief quotations embodied in critical articles and reviews.

Please purchase only authorized electronic editions, and do not participate in or encourage electronic piracy of copyrighted materials. Your support of the author's rights is appreciated.

For information regarding permission, please email BaBagilo, Inc at contact@babagilo.com or visit our website at www.babagilo.com

Also by
G.H. BABAGILO

A Storm of Cloaks Series

Introduction: *A Storm of Cloaks*

Book One: *Nestless Eagles*

Book Two: *A Duel of Feathers*

Book Three: *Tongues of Silk and Fire*

Book Four: *The Crown and the Cloak*

Awareness Books Collections

Grace of the Monarchs & Her Miraculous Journey

LOW EARTH
THE TREACHEROUS SEA
VERMILION ISLAND
GLACELAND
THE FROSTY REEF
THE SHATTERED GULF
THE WEREWOLF FOREST
MAGISOL
THE MAGICAL RAINBOW
THE WILD SEA
THE LONE WOLF HIGHLANDS
THE CRACK
THE PRAIRIE
THE GREAT RIVER
ELK PLAINS
THE GARDENS MOUNTAINS
THE GIANTS' FOREST
THE SKULLS SEA
BONE ISLES
THE RANGE OF HEROES
THE LIPS
THE STING MOUNTAINS
THE VENOMOUS OASES
THE SAND SEA
THE RED DESERT
THE PITCHFORK
THE ENDLESS FOREST
THE BLOODY RAVINE
THE RIVER OF FIRE
FIRRLANDIA

CONTENTS

1. The Drunken Half-Wits 1
2. A Guilty Cook 17
3. A Rare Team 25
4. A Clash from the Past 49
5. Investigation 57
6. A Short Revelation 75
7. The Drunken Maiden 93
8. Captain Eel 101
9. The Eagles' Shield 107
10. Everything on the Line 129
11. Unexpected Allies 149
12. Kisses and Blood 167
13. Magic in the Castle 185
14. Thunderstorm 207
15. Mourning and Hope 225
16. A Risky Plan 249
17. The Arena 271
About the Author 293

CHAPTER 1

THE DRUNKEN HALF-WITS

Captain Quint was standing at the bow, gazing with anxious eyes toward the north as dusk was falling fast. About three weeks had passed from the cursed night they had lost Rusty. Since then, he had returned to this very spot each and every night, waiting for their beloved first mate to emerge from the dark with soaking red hair. Yet he showed not.

Instead, a familiar scene occurred on an almost nightly basis. A ship would stop at the edge of the Frosty Reef, and when darkness fell, many lights would appear on its deck, and it would follow a small boat with a single guide-light deep into the Treacherous Sea.

Robin and his Ghosts watched those ships with frustrated eyes. They sailed into the most perilous waters and came out safely again, as though it was nothing more than a calm lake. That drove them mad.

The crew on the *Skulls Cleaver* always prided themselves on being bold pioneers and legendary sailors. Now they began to doubt their own myth.

Twilight arrived and Robin saw no lights. He had to make a painful decision.

"We are sailing east!" he commanded. The sound of his own words pierced his heart. He had to leave his best mate and brother behind.

"Aye, aye, Captain!" called the helmsman as he spun the ship's wheel. The men had grown tired of this painful routine.

Robin was on his way down to his cabin when the lookout bellowed from above.

"A ship is coming our way."

Quint hastened back to the deck and squinted to the north. The last dim light of the day was fading, but he could make out a single-masted boat sailing south across the Frosty Reef. Its white body protruded clearly from the dark blue.

He had seen this one in recent weeks. It didn't belong to the Navy; that much was for certain. His head exploded with questions, but he had no answers.

"Summon everyone!" he ordered. In a minute, everyone gathered on deck, including Alec, Lia, and Neal.

"My brothers!" the captain began, and only the ripples of the quiet ocean could be heard. "As we speak, a ship is heading out from the Treacherous Sea. It must have some valuable information. On my command, we shall approach from behind with stealth, surprise it, and seize it at all costs. Prepare for battle!"

His warriors began to buzz as though the *Cleaver* were a beehive. In a matter of minutes, all were fully armed and ready in their combat positions.

Darkness fell, and all eyes tracked the light of the ship. Half an hour later, the dark *Cleaver* crept up behind the small, white-hulled vessel.

Suddenly, two figures on deck were staring up at a giant shadow beside them. Their jaws dropped, as did their bottle of wine.

Before they could sound the alarm, fifteen warriors masked in black descended on ropes and landed around them. They seized the vessel in a matter of seconds. After a swift search, the Ghosts realized these two men were the only ones on board.

At once, they bound them and brought them aboard the *Skulls Cleaver*.

"Please, don't kill us…" one of them begged. "We only have a few coins."

The other man just shivered and gritted his teeth.

Robin stepped forward, surrounded by a ring of his shadows.

"Who are you?" His voice showed no patience and cut like a knife.

"My name is Mago," mumbled the older man with a shaking voice. "I am the captain of the *Drunken Maiden*, and this is my right hand, Lallo. We are simple traders from Scarlet Vale, selling wine to the northern people."

"Selling wine in the Treacherous Sea?" Robin asked sarcastically. His hand rested on the sword's hilt. "Do you take me for a fool?"

Mago and Lallo recoiled from his fury.

"How did you get through?" Robin demanded. "Who guided you in the water?" He skewered them with burning eyes, for he had no time for lies and deceit.

The two swayed like restless chickens that had been roasted alive.

"We sailed to an island in the north!" Lallo gushed in panic as his jumpy eyes watched Robin's sword.

"We only delivered wine barrels for the Bloody Shirts, nothing more. I speak the truth, Captain. I swear it!"

"How did two blockheads like yourselves manage to pass through the Treacherous Sea?" Quint drew his blade halfway, and the sound of cold steel quivered the two men's spines. "You'd better start talking, or these moments will be your last."

The two terrified sailors began babbling over each other at once.

"Silence!" Robin shouted. He glanced at Lallo. "You first."

"Thank you, Captain," he said politely, as though he were speaking to a king. "You are right—we could never travel through this deadly water without guidance. A safe path to the island is marked on a map—and in the water with a series of hidden buoys. As long as you don't stray, even fools like us can sail through these perilous seas."

Lallo wore a stupid smile on his face, trying to appease the angry captain.

Mago, however, shook his head, his eyes on the floor. "We are doomed now…" he murmured. "The Bloody Shirts will hunt us on land or sea."

"What is this island you speak of?" Robin ignored him, still pressing.

"It is a land of harsh wilderness filled with mountains and forests, quite similar to the Northern Kingdom," Mago replied before his foolish partner could flap his loose tongue. "We don't know the Bloody Shirts' business, Captain, for we were forbidden to set foot on the island. Yet, one thing is certain. They keep it secret and well-protected, and many ships are docked in the harbor."

Robin wore a discontented face, but he was more than pleased with the knowledge he had gleaned from these two.

"Helmsman, lead us back to the last waiting point!"

"Aye, aye, Captain!" the man answered.

"Neal! Prepare two boats with four men each. We will row to find the gap through the Frosty Reef."

"Aye, aye, sir!" said the Eel. His lively voice seemed ready for action.

"You two!" Robin snarled at the captives. "Right to my cabin. You'd better provide some real information on how to navigate to this island of yours."

***

About an hour later, two skiffs moved side by side through the inky water. Only a few stars glinted through the scattered clouds.

After many minutes of silence, Mago touched Robin's shoulder.

"There is the passage." He pointed to a shadow east of them. "Keep a hundred yards west of this rock."

Robin nodded. He noted the shattered chunks of ice accumulating on the northern side of the reef. He took a lantern and held it above his head. The rest probed with their oars to detect any danger lurking in the water.

"It's quite deep here, Captain," Neal said, hauling up the thin depth rope with its small lead weight. He counted off the knots. "Four fathoms. A ship can pass here safely."

And so they rowed through the opening and traversed the Frosty Reef for the first time. At the entrance to the Treacherous Sea, they stopped. Robin studied it with the eager eyes of a fresh sailor. He couldn't see far, yet he sighted some giant icebergs against the dark water.

"They are all marked on the map, Captain," Mago said behind him.

"Brilliant…" murmured Robin. Countless questions whirled in his mind. *Why are the Navy ships here in these waters? What's happening on this island?*

"The wizard must be informed about this," he mumbled, "but where I can find you, Elmagos?"

Suddenly he smelled a breath of wine behind his shoulder.

"In the North," said Mago indifferently.

Robin turned his head swiftly and stared at him with hard eyes.

Mago seemed confused by the reaction. "I'm sorry, Captain. I thought you asked where Elmagos was. He is in the Northern Kingdom as we speak. We sailed together some weeks ago."

Robin stared at him in disbelief. Within a moment, Mago's stinking breath transformed into a bunch of roses. He leaned closer.

Mago moved restlessly on his seat, and his eyes gazed at the captain like a terrified dog. He very much seemed to regret opening his mouth.

"Lallo!" Mago said with an anxious voice.

"Aye, aye, Captain!" he answered, then he hesitated and corrected himself with a weak smile at Robin. "I meant, aye, aye, Mago. There is only one captain here!"

Mago gave him a stare that could kill.

"When did we travel with Elmagos and the young man?" Mago said through clenched teeth. "Was it three weeks ago?"

"I think you are right," Lallo murmured, counting with his fingers.

By now, Captain Robin Quint had a broad grin on his face. *Nothing of this encounter with the two half-wits is a coincidence. The sea has sent me some unexpected guidance on my journey…*

"All right, men!" he said. "Now we know how to find the pass through the Frosty Reef. Let's head back to the ship. I suppose our two guests wouldn't mind a hearty dinner."

Mago and Lallo's tense faces sighed with relief.

***

Pozzo prepared another excellent feast that night, making the newcomers lick their fingers.

"Delicious!" Mago chirped as he chewed some crispy fish with a garlic sauce.

"Outstanding!" Lallo competed with Mago's compliment. He seemed much more comfortable than before.

The crew had grown used to Pozzo's flavorful dishes and couldn't imagine how they survived without him. He'd become the second most popular man on board, after Quint himself.

Dinner ended, and the two guests followed Robin to his cabin. They sat around the table, and he poured wine into their glasses.

"To Elmagos!" the captain toasted, and they drained the wine as if it were water.

For a long hour, he questioned them about their voyage with the wizard. Much calmer now that they were full of wine and food, they both answered freely.

"I heard them talking a few weeks ago," Lallo said with a conspiratorial voice. "Elmagos asked Evert to lead them quickly to Norvita before Prince Zigler arrives."

"Was that the reason they journeyed with you in the first place?" Robin asked. "So they could arrive before Zigler?"

"That's right, Captain. They spoke about investigating the Navy or something of that sort."

Robin's eyes pierced Mago, but they were sparkling. *Investigating the Navy,* he thought as his heart raced. *Perhaps the wizard suspects Zigler's actions...*

A sudden wave of hope flooded him, and his body became as light as a butterfly. At last, he had a chance for justice to prevail and to expose Zigler for who he truly was.

"Mago and Lallo!" Robin called gladly. "I was wrong to judge you harshly. We shall bring you back to your ship. However, you'd better not mention our meeting with anyone. If you do, I will find you both and take my vengeance."

"Our mouths will be sealed, Captain!" Mago promised, and Lallo nodded in agreement.

"One last thing…" said Robin with a serious voice.

"Whatever you ask, Captain," said Mago.

"I need you to take me to the Crescent Harbor aboard the *Drunken Maiden*." His words sounded unreal as they came out of his own mouth. After all, he had been the most wanted man in the North.

Mago's eyes squinted at the odd request. Clearly, it didn't make any sense to him. But Lallo, on the other hand, smiled widely.

"Of course, Captain! We are heading there anyway to load some more barrels, right, Mago? We can even bring you back to the ship, for we will return here to deliver more wine to the island."

Mago's face reddened as an ember. Robin could tell that he was envisioning all sorts of methods to torture Lallo and his big mouth as soon as they were alone.

Robin smiled, and Mago swallowed his saliva.

"Thank you, Lallo," Robin said easily. "That would be perfect."

At last, they retired from the cabin and went back up on deck. On their way up, Mago cleared his throat. "May I ask you one last question, Captain?"

Robin nodded.

A curious note filled his voice, and he asked. "Who are you?"

"I am Captain Quint!" he said without hesitation, and two jaws dropped to the floor.

***

When the *Skulls Cleaver* reached the *Drunken Maiden,* Robin summoned all his men to the dining chamber. Then he briefed them that he was about to sail to the Crescent Harbor, and the whole room went into turmoil.

"That's madness!" a voice called.

"Don't do it, Captain!" said another.

"They will catch you!" more voices snarled, and the mutterings continued to grow.

"Silence!" Robin shouted. "Do not let your spirits sink, my lions. This coming moment is a vital and hopeful step, for the last discoveries are too significant to be ignored. I must find Elmagos at all costs."

"We've already lost Rusty, and we can't lose you, Captain," Mello said. "You must be careful! What if they catch you? They will hang you on the spot!"

Robin understood their concerns, for it was a risky task indeed. Moments later, they all spilled out of the room and scattered back to their stations.

Alec and Lia saw him as he walked among the men.

"Captain! Captain!" Lia's voice trembled. "You must tell Elmagos about the Four Miracles Castle. You must let him know that the Bloody Shirts have taken everyone."

"I will," he snapped and bolted forward.

"What about our brothers and sisters?" she pleaded. "We can't abandon them on this Death Island!"

"The Bloody Shirts are vicious animals, sir!" Alec's eyes spat fire. "I am sure they are torturing them as we speak."

He stopped and gave them a sincere glance. "My dear Lia and Alec, I wish to do something about this island now, but I can't. It is a much bigger problem than that. The best thing I can do is inform Elmagos of what I know, and then decide on a plan. Let's pray we are not too late."

Robin left both disheartened as they stared at him hopelessly.

"We can't wait here and do nothing!" Lia called after him with a shaking voice.

Robin walked to the railing and looked down at the *Drunken Maiden* that was tied alongside.

"Where is Neal?" Robin asked curiously as Mello came near him.

"Ohhh," said Mello. "The poor man complained about his stomach. He said something about food poisoning and begged me not to bother him tonight."

"Hmm, I thought it was pretty good," said Robin with an odd gesture.

"Perhaps he is already missing you, Captain."

Both men burst into laughter. Moments later, Mello searched for a rope but couldn't find it. When he glanced over the railing, a line was dangling down to the white boat.

"That's strange..." the Sea Ghost mumbled. "Well, Captain, the rope is ready for you." He caught himself quickly. "I didn't mean it in that regard."

Robin gave him a stern glance as he climbed down to the *Drunken Maiden,* where Mago and Lallo were waiting for him.

"Captain Mago," he smiled. "The *Drunken Maiden* is yours to sail. I am just a passenger here."

CHAPTER 2

A GUILTY COOK

While the *Drunken Maiden* sailed east toward the Crescent Harbor, Pozzo finished up his duties in the kitchen.

As happened each day, the crew heaped praise on his cooking. For the first time in his bumpy life, he had mastered something and took tremendous pride in it. Soon enough, the Sea Ghosts embraced him as a brother, and the *Skulls Cleaver* felt like home.

Pozzo made a bowl of hot stew for Neal after Mello had told him he was unwell. But when he opened the door to Neal's cabin, his mouth fell open. The Eel was standing on his head against the wall, gazing at him upside down.

"Top of the evening to you, master cook!" he spoke lively, still with his head on the floor.

Pozzo tried to read his lips but instead got dizzy.

"The soup was remarkable tonight. I wouldn't mind another serving." Neal flipped in the air, landed on his feet, grabbed the dish from his friend, and gulped it loudly.

"It's a stew, not a soup!" Pozzo sounded offended, and he darted a suspicious glimpse at him. "You seem vigorous to me. I expected to find you sick in bed."

"Ahhhh...delicious!" Neal sighed with a smile. Then he ordered, "Close the door."

Pozzo found himself obeying at once. That was the power of the oily tongue he hated, but at the same time admired. Now he sat on his bed, and Neal threw at him a sly glance.

"Pozzo...shipmate..." He spoke with a familiar silky tone, one that invited many troubles. "Our golden chance has finally come, my friend. Captain Quint is heading to the North now, and no one is in his cabin. I say we take Rollo's map and necklace, lower a boat to the water, and be on our way to the Bone Isles. There we can find a ship easily and sail for the largest treasure ever!"

Neal had a note of cheerfulness in his voice, as though he was expecting enthusiasm, but no response came.

Pozzo sat on his bed and stared at his knees in misery.

This is the story of my worthless life, he thought. *Anytime something good happens to me, the "golden opportunity" rears its ugly face, and then I'm back in my troubles again.*

"I see!" Neal's cunning voice woke him out of his thoughts. "Pozzo grew a conscience. The gold must not be as important as it used to be."

"It's not that..." Pozzo's voice turned apologetic. "It's just...at last I belong to something. If I do it, the captain and the men would never forgive me."

A silence fell in the room. The Eel frowned. Apparently, he hadn't expected this kind of reaction, particularly not from Pozzo, whose lust for gold was unmatched.

Then the cook showed a fracture in his already weak armor.

"But I would be lying if I said my heart does not crave Rollo's treasure."

Neal simply nodded, smiling at his friend.

"I am happy for you, Pozzo. You are a true shipmate and very well deserve to serve on the *Skulls Cleaver.*"

Pozzo's eyes widened. He had expected Neal's smooth tongue to try and convince him. Instead, the man stood up, whistled a famous pirate song, and pulled out a leather pack from under his bed, making each of his motions noticeable.

"All right, shipmate. We had some adventures together. You will be missed."

He hugged the frozen cook.

Poor Pozzo breathed like a donkey, not knowing what to do. Suddenly, thrilling visions of adventures, treasures, and exquisite rum flooded his mind. He could almost taste it on his tongue.

"Wait!" Pozzo called in a panic. "What are you doing, going like that by yourself? It's dangerous out there, and you need a loyal seadog by your side."

Neal's eyes measured him. "Before you volunteer, I want you to understand one thing. My plan is to bring Rollo's treasure and divide it equally among all the fine men on this ship. I swore an oath to the *Skulls Cleaver,* and I will keep my word."

Pozzo gave him an astonished gaze and wondered if it was the same sneaky eel he knew.

"Without Captain Quint's help, I couldn't have solved Rollo's riddle," Neal declared in gratitude. "But he is fully wrapped up with all the recent events. The reason I am rushing after the treasure now is to seize it before the Bloody Shirts do. If they put their hands on it first, they would be impossible to stop."

"Pozzo is waiting for your command, Captain Eel!" he declared with a proud smile.

***

After packing their bags with food, water, and clothing, Neal sneaked to the captain's cabin and came out with Rollo's map and necklace. Robin Quint never locked his room from his men—a sign of the utter trust they all had in each other.

Ten minutes later, Pozzo went up deck, carrying a tray.

"Hey, come over here!" he called, and the three Sea Ghosts on the night shift gathered at the bow.

"Here is some tea and lemon cake I baked for tomorrow's breakfast." He winked at them.

"I bless the day you arrived on our ship, master cook," said one. The rest nodded in agreement while gulping the tasty warm liquid.

Pozzo smiled and turned his head away. He couldn't look at their eyes, for a pang of painful guilt pierced him. It was mental torture to stay beside them, but he had to follow his captain's plan.

While the four men were drinking their tea, Neal kept busy. He lowered a small skiff at the stern. Once it touched the surface, he climbed down the rope and rowed southwest. A hundred yards from the *Cleaver*, he stopped and waited for his friend.

By now, the guards returned to their posts. Next, Pozzo asked one of them to replace him in the kitchen tomorrow morning so he could attend to sick Neal.

At last, he dashed below deck, entered Quint's cabin, and climbed out of the window. He slid into the water like a water snake and swam to the boat even though he could not yet see it.

"Over here..." Neal whispered with a smile and helped him climb over the side. "Welcome aboard, shipmate."

Pozzo covered himself with a blanket, took the oars, and together they began rowing until the *Cleaver's* shadow was out of sight. Soon after, they set the mast and opened the sail.

"Steady as she goes, First Mate!" Neal called proudly, as though he commanded a warship. "Southwest to the Pirates' Islands."

The hair on their backs rose with excitement, and they grinned as widely as the crescent moon above.

CHAPTER 3

A RARE TEAM

In the Southlands, near Capana, Niro and Tashunko went through the Wilkens' dark house and ran upstairs, each to their own room. They took off their dresses and slipped back into their regular clothes, but they didn't dare to light a candle, for their rooms were adjacent to the back patio.

But they couldn't hide forever. Curious like a cat, Niro peeked an eye behind the curtain and scanned the garden below. A group of a dozen maidens was sitting around Edelin and Olivia, roaring with laughter.

Their faces seemed familiar, and seconds later, it dawned on him: the girls from the lake.

One of them was telling what had happened, and everyone around her was in tears.

Ronald, Ganix, and Marc sat beside them and were busting their guts as she performed the moment when Lady Troll hurled the two boys into the water.

The girl knows how to tell a story; I'll give her that much, Niro thought, and even he chuckled behind the window.

After several hours, the guests all went home, and Niro and Tashunko were able to get some troubled sleep. Dawn came far too soon, and Niro and Tashunko stood in the field, exhausted but both glad the crawling night was over.

A moment later, Edelin approached with a wide smile on her face. "No dresses this morning, girls?"

Niro and Tashunko prepared themselves for a long day of harassment.

"Don't you worry, boys, that was my final teasing," she promised while stretching, but they gave her a doubtful gaze. A sneaky smile crept upon her face. "However, I must inform you that as your loyal teammate, you earned yourselves many admirers at that maidens' school."

Tashunko shook his head, and Niro dismissed her with a snort.

"I swear it!" Edelin said defensively. "I am not lying. They even invited you to a party they are about to have a week from today."

Both the boys acted indifferently. The painful humiliation from last night was as fresh as the dew itself.

"Ask Olivia if you don't believe me!" she said with an offended voice.

"It doesn't matter!" the Black Tongue snapped. "Even if it's true, you won't find me within a mile of that Lady Troll. I learned my lesson."

"That's the best thing, Tashunko!" Edelin said. "She won't be there. In fact, she is supposed to travel to the Stallion Hills for a few days. That's why they're throwing the party."

"Well..." Niro said with a formal voice. "If the giant woman won't be around, we should protect our new fans."

The three teammates burst into laughter, but then a familiar voice yelled from behind them.

"Planning another adventure, Lady Nira?"

Ganix approached with a rare smile on his face, the remnants of the hysterical laughs from the night before.

"No more adventures for me, sir!" Niro answered swiftly. But none of them seemed to believe his statement, for his sparkling sapphire eyes spoke otherwise.

They headed to the practice ground after their usual warm-up with Ganix. The battle training began with attacking moving targets with different weapons.

Marc showed them a small taste of it. He raced down the field, drew two swords, and slashed the dummies at close quarters. Next, he flung knives at the midrange and shot arrows at the far marks—all in swift, decisive motions.

While practicing the battle training, the two masters polished their blade techniques.

During the afternoon, they drilled defense—running and hitting their targets while evading and blocking flying arrows and knives.

The long hours turned into days, and the two Ghosts nipped at their heels, not letting go. At last, the three reached their final evaluation.

They were attacked from short-, mid-, and long-distance, and they had to minimize their wounds. At the same time, they needed to attack their foes with swords, knives, and arrows.

Edelin went first. She had been struck eight times by weapons before she killed all her targets. It was considered a good result.

Tashunko was hit six times only, and got loud applause, even from Ganix himself.

If the Black Tongue was a mighty warrior and undisputed champion in one-on-one combat, and Edelin was second-to-none in rapid shooting and flinging knives, Niro was the king of battle training.

Over these final days of practice, he had left them all in awe. His ability to sense the big picture and prioritize his targets in a split second was exceptional. The two masters and his friends seemed eager to watch him in action.

The test began, and he raced down the field. Against everyone's prediction, he evaded the close-quarters foes and hit the mid-range ones that threw spears and knives at him. Using his swift shooting technique, he struck the far marks and eliminated the deadliest first. Last, he demonstrated his highly skilled fighting with two swords at a time, attacking and blocking like lightning. By the time he had struck all the dummies, no weapon had hit him. Further, it had only taken him half the time of the others.

No one cheered. Instead, an utter silence followed. The lad stood with his eyes shut, replaying his actions in slow motion.

"Niro!" Ronald boomed. He had been sitting under an oak tree and watching the whole time.

"Come, all of you. I brought you some fruit." His eyes were still fixed on the boy.

Once they were all gathered, Ronald was focused entirely on Niro.

"How did you do that?" He tossed him an apple together with a strange gaze.

Niro took a hard bite, and it crunched in the silence.

"You heard him," Ganix said with an annoyed note in his voice. "How did you move like that?"

"I just did!" Niro replied sharply, not liking the way all of them were eying him.

"What?" He snapped at Tashunko, who stared at him and shrugged his shoulders.

"Niro," Marc said with his steady voice. "The reason we are still staring at you is because of your remarkable performance. It was beyond words. To not get hit in battle training had been considered unthinkable—until today." He smiled at him in wonder.

The lad stared at the ground and let it sink into his mind.

"I felt that everything was happening in slow-motion," he mumbled. "I followed my instincts, and my body moved before they shot their arrows. It felt timeless and effortless. I have no better words to explain..."

Ronald exchanged glances with Marc, who in turn looked at Ganix. Niro could tell that this explanation was too vague for the two practical-minded trainers. Although they were excited about Niro's outcome, they seemed frustrated.

Ganix, who believed in techniques, preparation, and precise methods above all, swayed restlessly under the branches. Lunch came just in time for Niro, who started to feel annoyed by the awkward behavior around him. He rushed uphill, not waiting for his teammates.

"Do you believe him?" Ganix asked when the three masters left alone.

"I do," Marc said at once.

"As do I," Ronald added. "His eyes didn't lie."

"Both of you watched him!" snapped Ganix. "It is impossible to move like that. He knew where the arrows and knives would hit and avoided them with ease!"

The winemaker smiled. "Sounds like magic..."

"Well...he is Elmagos's favorite boy, is he not? Do you think the wizard taught him some tricks?"

"No." Ronald stood to his feet. "I think the boy found magic within himself."

***

After lunch, Marc walked beside Niro. "Do you mind doing it again?"

He stared at him, confused. "Do what?"

"The battle training."

"Why?"

"I want to learn more about what you do on the field. Imagine what I can teach the Ghosts if I can break down your success. All will benefit from that—except for our enemies, of course." He laughed, and his eyes sparkled like a child.

"Sure!" Niro knew how dedicated of a trainer he was, and he wanted to help him. Nonetheless, the three men's stunned reactions had made him doubt himself now.

"Excellent!" Marc said cheerfully and instructed everyone to take their positions in the maze.

Niro was standing there, but the thoughts whirled in his mind, trying to strategize his way on the battlefield.

"Begin!" Marc shouted. The lad sprinted, slashed the nearby targets, and shot swiftly both near and far.

"Stop!" the master called. Ten dummies had fallen. It was still a fast time, yet Niro had been struck six times.

They all gathered under the oak. Marc was writing some notes, and Niro gasped for air, wiping the sweat from his face.

"All right," Marc began, "the speed was impressive. You struck the far targets swiftly, but the ones to hit you over and over again were the knives at the mid-range."

Over the next few hours, the team practiced shooting arrows on wooden plates that were thrown in the air.

They all did very well and teased each other with names. The tension of the late morning dissipated like a mist on a sunny day.

An hour before sunset, the three huddled together with their trainers and Ronald.

Marc and Ganix summarized the week of battle training. They talked about the tactics and methods and suggested ways to improve the competitor's skills.

When done, they asked each one if they had something to add.

Edelin advised holding the bow with few arrows in the hand when attacking the far targets, and they all agreed it could improve the speed of shooting while running.

Tashunko thought that during a large-scale skirmish, fighting with two swords would be better and deadlier than a sword and a shield.

When Niro's turn came, he suggested respectfully, "I think we should put less emphasis on planning and more on sensing the battlefield."

A profound silence followed, and the tension from the morning seeped back into the air.

The eyes around him didn't seem to grasp the meaning, so he searched for the right words.

"What I meant was, every battle situation is different, so you can't prepare for all scenarios that might happen. Knowing tactics is useful, but it's not the most important thing, in my opinion."

Ganix's voice was sarcastic and impatient. "Then name the most significant thing, master Niro."

"Quietness…stillness. Not having a single thought in your mind. Just being present and aware of everything you do. When I was calm, I knew what to do without thinking about it."

Ganix probed him with squinting eyes. "If it was so easy, how come you got smacked six times during the second test?"

"Because I doubted myself, and many voices filled my mind. Can I do it again? What do the others think of me? How many arrows could I block? All sorts of distractions came through, rather than trusting my ability and being fully there with all my senses."

Marc smiled. "That is an excellent, candid answer! Something real that we can all apply."

"This is not a practical method," Ganix muttered. "It was pure luck!"

Everyone heard Ganix's words, including Niro, who sat quietly and kept his composure.

"I don't agree!" Marc snapped back. "You are overreacting, Ganix."

"Sir…" Niro said with a genuine voice. "With your approval, I would like to do the test again."

Marc clearly didn't like the idea, but he relented when Ronald nodded.

Now the boy marched to the middle of the field for the third attempt that day. The men were ready in the trenches with targets attached high above their heads. The rest were preparing their bows, knives, and spears for the final practice of the day.

Niro stood still as a rock, sensing all sounds around him. His heartbeat slowed as he held a bow and some arrows in his left hand and a sword in his right.

"Begin!" Marc bellowed, and Niro bolted like a racehorse on a track.

He slashed the closest marks to him with his blade first, then leaped and rolled on the ground, evading the knives from the mid-range foes.

Then, he kneeled and hit the targets with three swift arrows. As they fell, he bounced like a cat, threw a knife at a close target, and then struck the far ones with his bow while changing direction from left to right.

"Stop!" Marc shouted, but no one heard him. The men who held the targets in the trenches were cheering together with Edelin and Tashunko. A flawless performance again.

The tall Ghost joined the applause as he gave Ganix a critical look.

"I know... I know..." his friend mumbled in disbelief. At once, the stocky master sprinted through the field and lifted Niro up on his broad shoulders.

"Allow me to present the king of the battlefield, Master Niro!" Ganix cried, and all roared with laughter.

"Early dinner at the garden!" Ronald announced with a smile.

They all walked up the hill—except for Niro, who Ganix insisted on carrying all the way to Ronald's home.

Eating before the sun had set was refreshing. On the back terrace, the host and his guests sat around a loaded table. The red sunset painted the clouds with purple and gold, nourishing their souls while the tasty food made their stomachs sing.

Suddenly Ganix stood and raised his cup. "To Niro, who taught me today an unforgettable lesson in humility!"

Everyone cheered.

"To the brilliant Southern Team members, each one with their own exceptional qualities!" Marc bellowed, and all slammed their hands on the thick wooden table.

"And to our three fierce and beloved masters," Edelin said, "who are second to none in Low Earth. Deep gratitude from the bottom of our hearts!" Her turquoise eyes sparkled at them, and there was no doubt that she meant each and every word. The two boys stood beside her and bowed with respect to the trainers.

Soon after, they indulged in honey cakes and warm apple pies while Ronald poured them some tea.

"From tomorrow, Marc and Ganix will strengthen your weaknesses," said Ronald.

The three were surprised, as they thought that the test today meant their training was over.

Ganix noticed their expressions. "We must also train you on body strength and night skills!" he added with an unsatisfied voice. "Always strive to become better. The day you think you know everything is the day of your demise."

His voice was serious, and the young contenders took his wisdom deep into their minds.

"Edelin!" Olivia called from inside the house. "Don't forget about the party. We must be going soon!"

The princess jumped to her feet as though someone had spilled hot soup on her.

"I completely forgot about it!" she admitted nervously. "Come on you two, up, up, to your room! Both of you stink like pigs. You need to wash."

But the boys were lazily drinking their tea, with no hurry at all. Niro sniffed himself and then Tashunko, who gave him a baffled stare.

"I think these two pigs smell like lilies," he said with the most annoying voice. "We don't even need to bathe."

"Is that right?" Edelin shrieked like a dragon, and her fair cheeks began to redden.

The two had heard that tone before. It was just before she turned into a thunderstorm.

They exchanged a terrified glance, and before her fire could roast them alive, they hastened like young rabbits up to their rooms.

Edelin gave a satisfying gesture to the three masters, who enjoyed the show. "This significant skill, I learned from my mother!" she winked, and they burst into laughter.

***

An hour later, two clean, handsome young men appeared downstairs. They were dressed neatly, and the long, wild hair that usually hung down in their faces was brushed tight behind their napes.

Edelin wore a scarlet dress on her fair skin. Her turquoise eyes gleamed like two precious stones, spreading a royal glow around the room. She was stunning, like a red rose under the twilight.

The two boys watched her with their tongues out as she walked down the staircase. Seeing her every day with her sweaty ponytail and dusty pants made them forget how beautiful she was. For long weeks they had felt like she was just another boy in the team. Tonight, however, Edelin was the princess she had always resented being, and now she seemed happy to embrace it.

She reached her smiling teammates and slid her arms between their elbows, dragging them to the backyard.

Olivia joined them on the terrace, wearing a flowing white dress. Her long, golden hair rested on her back, and her dark blue eyes glinted at Edelin and the two young men. At once, she grabbed Edelin's arm and whispered something, sneaking a smile back to Tashunko.

"Olivia!" her father said. "Enjoy the night, but don't come too late!"

She ran and gave him a kiss on the cheek, melting his heart like butter.

"Don't worry about us ladies, father," she said with a sly voice. "You should be more concerned about the boys!"

The masters laughed as they remembered the last time Niro and Tashunko came back from the lake.

"Let's go, girls!" Olivia smiled, and the lads growled from behind. "The school's maidens always throw the best parties."

When they walked away from her father's eyes, she halted and dashed to the stone staircase leading to the basement.

"What are you doing?" Edelin puzzled behind her.

"Tell the boys to come; I need their help!"

"Psssstt!" The princess signed to her teammates. Olivia opened the iron door to the basement, and they all went inside. Then she closed the door and lit a lantern.

"Wow!" Niro's eyes grew wide. "This is huge!"

The underground chamber was as large as the entire mansion and packed with thousands of wine barrels.

"Go on, what are you waiting for?" Olivia stood there like a supervisor, crossing her hands on her chest. Niro and Tashunko stared at her, all confused.

"Pick up a barrel, each one of you. We need it for the party!" she commanded the two boys, who didn't like the idea at all.

"I heard you are fast and strong, so let's move quickly before my father discovers us stealing his babies. Otherwise, you will meet his nasty temper!"

At once, together they lifted a cask of Wilken's wine onto their backs. It was a heavy load, but the thought of mad Ronald bolting into the basement intimidated them even more. They climbed up the stairs and ran into the fields as light-footed as two gazelles.

The two maidens strolled and giggled uphill toward the ridge while the boys cursed and plodded under the weighty burden. Rather than enjoying a relaxing night, they were dripping sweat after washing themselves not an hour ago.

"Is it far?" The Black Tongue gasped impatiently as Olivia chuckled and Edelin bit her lip, trying not to laugh.

"Not at all; it is quite close." She winked at the princess.

"At least we won't have to carry these damn barrels on our way back!" Niro forced his determined legs uphill. "Even if that means I have to drink the whole barrel myself."

Moments later, they reached the crest. They continued on the path for ten minutes until music and voices came to their ears.

"Finally!" Tashunko smiled. The maidens giggled with excitement as they got closer to the school's yard.

Hundreds of lanterns dangled on the trees and illuminated the entire ground. Girls and boys were playing cheerful music with flutes and drums, while others were dancing and laughing all around.

"I thought this was a school for maidens!" Niro whispered to Olivia as he watched many youths about their age.

"It is!" she cackled. "These young men are from the school not far from ours. Sorry to disappoint if you thought for a moment that you would be the only boys at the party."

Edelin laughed, but Niro and Tashunko cared for nothing except putting down the damn barrels on the ground.

As they marched behind the two young ladies, many of the figures eyed them with curiosity.

Edelin and Olivia mingled briskly among the maidens, who all admired their beauty and their dresses.

The two lads stood behind an empty table, studying the faces around them. They recognized some girls from that unforgettable day in the lake.

Most of the boys gathered in one area, talking between themselves and darting bitter glances at the newcomers. For whatever reason, they didn't like these two at all.

"Forget about them, brother!" Niro placed his hand on his friend's tense back. "We are here to enjoy as always!"

He handed the Black Tongue a glass of red, and a mischievous smile spread on his face. A moment after, he jumped on the table and announced:

"My dear young lords and ladies. My friend and I carried a heavy load of the finest wine. Let's share it together and make sure that there is not one drop left. The bar is officially open!"

Loud cheers and clapping came around them as Niro stepped down. The young maidens rushed toward the handsome youngsters, who filled their cups with excitement.

However, not one of the boys who sat around the fire came to the bar. Instead, their resentment grew stronger with each passing moment. Watching the girls running and smiling around these two outsiders seemed to drive them mad.

The wine flowed, and the music played. Some of the maidens invited Tashunko and Niro to dance, while the young men kept glaring at them with bitterness.

"Why don't you put your dresses on?" one of them shouted as the group around him chortled like boars.

"I will gladly do so if you promise to dance with me," Niro answered back, and everybody laughed, including some of the boy's friends.

Finally, the two took a break from dancing and sat down at one of the tables.

"Why do these boys look at us like that?" Tashunko asked one of the girls. "They don't even know us."

"Oh, don't pay attention to them!" she dismissed. "They are all spoiled brats, sons of great lords and affluent families, full of pride and self-importance. They think they can disrespect people, and yet they expect everyone to bow and treat them with honor. Especially the three over there in the circle!" She pointed at a few figures who had been staring at them the whole night.

Niro gazed at them but couldn't see their faces, for they were sitting in the darkness.

"They were the members of the Southern Team for the last two years before you three replaced them." She added with a smile. Niro, Tashunko, and Edelin exchanged dark glances.

"Let me guess..." Niro said. "These boys are from Capana Royalty Academy... Jeffry Lom and his loyal puppies. Now I see where the resentment comes from!" he muttered and gave his old rival a long, intense glare.

CHAPTER 4

A CLASH FROM THE PAST

"Hey, you three!" one of the shadows around the campfire called. At once, Niro recognized the pompous voice of Jeffry Lom. "You should compete at the fools' dancing tourney, not the Wizards' Game!"

The boys around him roared with laughter.

Edelin's and Tashunko's cheeks reddened like wine, and they both jumped to their feet, but the sapphire-eyed lad was gazing at Jeffry in amusement. He stood up calmly and winked at his companions.

"Relax, my friends. Don't lose your poise. Let's see if I can play a bit with this skunk."

The two smiled. They knew Niro had a cunning mind like no other. None who knew him desired to be his enemy.

He poured drinks into three cups and grinned. "Let's greet our new friends!" he called out, and the surrounding tables cheered.

With a sneaky smile, he motioned for his teammates to join him, and they all headed to the boys' group. A sudden silence fell on the busy yard. The music stopped, and all were watching in anticipation of what would happen next.

"My lords!" Niro bowed slightly as he handed each one a cup.

They glared at him with confusion.

"The dancing fools would be honored to receive some useful advice from three fine champions like yourselves!" he announced, and everyone clapped. The gathered crowd admired Niro's kind gesture toward the boys.

"I will give you only one counsel!" Jeffry said, his voice full of spite. "Stay home and save the South from the worst disgrace ever in the Wizards' Game!"

Jeffry's words hit strong, and the murmurs grew around him. He must have felt the crowd tilt in his favor because the tall young man went for the kill.

"Look at you! Are you really stupid enough to believe you have a chance?" He circled them with a loathing expression on his face. "A spoiled princess from the North, who thinks her beauty should be enough. You need to offer much more than that." He chortled and brushed her hair.

Edelin was about to jump up and attack him like a mad dog, but Niro, who stood at the middle, clasped her wrist firmly, grounding her to the spot.

"Ah yes," Jeffry continued, "the orphan from the repulsive Four Miracles shelter. A place that rats and dogs wouldn't even call home. Everyone in the South knows he's been chosen only because he is Elmagos's little puppy."

Niro's heart was racing, but he calmed himself swiftly. *This bastard is indeed vicious,* he thought to himself.

"But the last and worst of this useless team is this savage creature!" Jeffry pointed at Tashunko. "A member of a brutal tribe, traitors and cursed savages who have no culture. They all need to be chained!"

Niro held the Black Tongue with all his strength, but he sensed the boiling blood gushing in his friend's veins. There was no force in the world to stop the mighty savage now. He leaped high in the air and kicked Jeffry's face.

The young lord flew straight on his back, and the boys drew back in fear of Tashunko's wrath. Niro wrapped his arms around his friend, trying to calm him down as the murmurs grew around them.

"I've had enough of these people and their party!" Tashunko snapped to his teammates with a voice full of pain and bleeding pride.

"I told you!" Jeffry shrieked as he sat on the ground, licking his wounds like a whipped dog. "I told you all that he is a wild animal!"

"Stay where you are," Niro whispered to his brother, his eyes like frozen knives. "We can't run away every time someone mocks us as an orphan, a princess, or a savage. We face it right here and right now. Trust me!"

He shoved Tashunko aside; then he turned around to face the crowd. The murmurs stopped at once.

"My dear friends!" Niro announced. "This bitter swine here called us all sorts of names: orphan, princess, savage. Ask yourselves, why would someone treat people he doesn't know with such viciousness? Why would anyone with any brains at all doubt and criticize the Great Wizard's decision? For that, I have one answer, which is the real truth. He must be a fool, full of fear and hate, and certainly unwise. After meeting you and your teammates, I can see clearly why the Southern Team lost all those years."

Jeffry sprang to his feet and growled, held by his two companions. Before he could say a word, Niro glared at him with blazing eyes.

"Down, you miserable dog, and listen carefully!" Niro barked. "I will take this beautiful princess of the North, and the mighty savage warrior of the Black Tongue Clan, any day of the week against you and your rotten team."

Niro put his arms around his friends, and together they returned to the cheering crowd.

"Are you ready to put your words to the test, or will you walk away like a coward?!" Jeffry screamed from behind, and a silence fell again.

"We are ready for anything," Niro said as he turned around. He spoke with confidence, but Tashunko and Edelin didn't seem comfortable with the way this was going.

Jeffry drew himself up tall. "We shall have five little contests between us. Each one presents a different skill. The team to win the most will be the champion!"

"Agreed!" Niro answered at once. "What is the bet?"

"The winning group will represent the South in the Wizards' Game!" Jeffry declared, and his lapdogs snorted with excitement.

"And if you lose?" Niro asked coolly.

Both Edelin and Tashunko gaped at him in disbelief, as if they never expected him to take such a bet seriously.

"Ask what you want, and you shall have it!" Jeffry gave an arrogant smirk. "You know very well who my father is."

"I heard Lord Henry Lom owns plenty of farmland near the Sea Forest."

"Yes, that's right."

"When you are defeated—" Niro raised his voice, which made Jeffry snarl, "—the ranches south of Fluky Village, where many of the Black Tongues work, will be given to the tribe."

"You coward!" the highborn barked at him with a purple face. "You demand too much just so you can escape the bet! It's not fair!"

"It's just a little price for your pride!" Niro answered, and everyone laughed. "Besides, there is no way that you will lose to a princess, a savage, and an orphan, right?"

Jeffry glared at him with more hate than ever. "Agreed!" he shouted.

"What are you doing?" Tashunko snarled under his breath.

"Are you out of your mind?" Edelin grabbed Niro's wrist and shook him. "Who do you think you are, taking this reckless bet on our behalf?!" Fury and panic choked her voice, and beads of sweat dripped from her forehead. "All the hell and training I went through could be in vain… What have you done?"

Niro gazed at his furious friends. "To be honest, I am not sure why I did it. But I know one thing for certain: we can beat these guys. This would be our final and most important test as a team, and if we don't win, perhaps we shouldn't have been chosen in the first place." He looked at his friends earnestly. "Cast your doubts and trust your training. Let's show these bastards what a princess, an orphan, and a savage are made of!"

Niro raised his hand in the air, and they all joined him. Their jaws clenched like rocks, and their burning gazes were determined like never before. They were ready for the battle of their lives.

CHAPTER 5

INVESTIGATION

When Elmagos left the Cloak Castle in Norvita, it was an hour before sunset. Like the wind, he galloped on his steed, heading south along the winding river toward the Garland Mountains.

The first night he slept in an old inn. It was precisely what he hoped for, untended and quiet and largely empty. At dawn, he was back on his saddle.

The sun was shining on fields of vibrant flowers and green grass, and Elmagos's spirit rose with it. He forgot how beautiful the North was during springtime.

After visiting some villages and picking up many conversations, he resumed traveling along the Cedar

Woods River. The colorful plains turned into rough, mountainous terrain. Elmagos tracked the river and found himself in a narrow valley between two mountain ridges.

On his right, massive green cedars mantled the lower western slopes, and on his left, maples painted the eastern slope in scarlet. High above them, ashen granite peaks shot up from the white snow blanket.

For long hours, the wizard rode, allowing himself only a few short breaks. His eyes scanned the breathtaking scenery, and this untarnished land embraced him like her first lover. Here, there was no sign of men, and yet this terrain was full of life.

Herds of elk and deer grazed on the lush grass that grew on the valley floor. Birds were singing ancient songs and woodpeckers drummed their heads into the bark of trees. On a pile of boulders at the river's edge, a family of bears splashed in the water with their fierce claws and hunted fish. A sudden cry from an eagle came from above and cut Elmagos's thoughts like a sharp knife.

At last, the vale grew wider, and his keen eyes caught a glimpse of an Army camp veiled beside a bunch of hills beneath the Garland Mountains. Elmagos galloped along the shoreline of a lake then ducked into the forest to spy on the camp.

Many Gray Wolf banners flapped over tall wooden palisades, but the hundreds of soldiers within wore red shirts.

So the Royal Army has turned into the Zigler's Bloody Shirts, he thought.

Hours later, he left under the cover of the night. The next days he encircled the Garland Mountains from the south until he reached the Golden Woods boundary. There, between the endless blond birches and the foothills, he noted scattered camps and thousands of Bloody Shirts.

For long days, the wizard hastened his horse through the vast Elk Plains and toward the Snowy Mountains. He visited many inns, probing and asking for strange events, but no answers came. The people volunteered no useful information and gave the prying stranger nasty glances. Some faces seemed to hound him, appearing at one inn after another, and Elmagos knew he was being followed. The Queen's words echoed in his head: *Zigler's spies are everywhere.* All the villages and towns along his journey confirmed what Enya had told him—the serpent prince controlled the entire Northern Kingdom. *This is not the same North I had known, but an unfriendly, cursed realm.*

Frustrated and weary, he decided on the shortest route to his final destination, the Navy Fortress. He galloped westward along the White Snake River, passed through Norvita's Gap, and headed northwest toward the Lukos Watchers. Sadness seized his spirit as he rode through ghost towns and lines of folks fleeing the settlements on the Shattered Gulf coastline.

As though we don't have enough on our plates, now we must add these White Wolf savages to our long list of threats.

The sunset sky had been painted with purple and gold when Elmagos arrived at the Navy Fortress. To his surprise, the gate was opened immediately.

"Welcome, my wizard!" an officer greeted him with an oily tongue. "Why do we deserve such an honor?"

They were expecting me here.

"Save your flattery for your senior commander; I have no use of it!" Elmagos snapped at the short man and gave him an icy gaze. He had grown tired of politeness, dishonesty, and betrayal. The time had come to discover what had been going on. "You know why I am here. The

Navy is under investigation, and you had better provide me the facts I need, and much more."

The officer was shocked by the wizard's intensity and had no option but to obey his demands. After two days in the fortress, Elmagos left no stone unturned. However, soon enough, he realized they had prepared for his visit. But despite the missing important documents and the evasive answers, he was able to grasp some significant facts.

On the third night, while all the Navy officers were eating dinner, Elmagos sneaked out of his room. Eyes had been spying on him from every corner ever since his arrival, but now he had to shake them off. His horse was ready for him at the stable, and moments later, he bolted out of the fortress and into the dark.

The chilly night lashed his face as he sped downhill on the road. When he reached a sharp curve, he entered the pine trees on his right and hid in the shadows.

Not a minute went by, and a clatter of hooves echoed in the distance. Three shadows on horses were speeding eastward, searching in vain for their target.

Now that the leeches were off his back, the wizard headed south through the crowded slopes of pines and toward the distant lights of the harbor.

At the foot of the hill, he stood silent in the cover of the trees. His frustrated eyes scanned the Crescent Road, but it was still too crowded for his taste.

I better leave the horse nearby, he thought. *The spies will search for a horseman.*

Like a shadow, he trotted behind some buildings and entered the stable from the alley. There he left his mount, rushing south on the main road toward Romi's Inn.

He needed to talk to his trusted friend and get his counsel. Romi, once a captain in the Royal Fleet, knew much about many affairs—his ears were always open to all sorts of conversations in his tavern.

However, as Elmagos approached the place, he froze. The front porch was crowded, and among the people were some suspicious faces.

"Damn!" He turned back with frustration, not taking the risk of putting Romi's family in danger. On his way back, Elmagos halted.

"The well…" he mumbled with sparkling eyes. He then dashed down a dirt alley that ran behind the inn.

Two drunken men and a blind beggar were the only figures he came across. In a blink of an eye, he crept through an opening in the rear fence and entered the inn's back yard.

Elmagos made his way through weeds and thorny bushes when he came upon two growling dogs. Their green eyes glared at him, and saliva dripped from their mouths. They were ready to attack the intruder, but the wizard stared at the dogs calmly. His eyes turned pale like the moon, glowing at them from above.

At once, they lowered their heads, wagged their tails, and crawled to his feet.

He glanced up at the inn. The dim yellow light spilled through the windows, and trees grew along the back wall. At last, his eyes found what he'd come for. Elmagos stepped toward a round stone well with a smile on his face. Moss grew between the stones, and twisted vines curled like snakes into the pitch-black hole.

Nothing's changed, he thought, surveying the pitched wooden roof above the well and the dangling rope.

Besides the dogs wagging their tails, all was still. And so he slid inside and climbed down an iron ladder into the dark well.

"One, two, three, four, five, six," Elmagos counted the rungs. Next, he groped the surface on his right and found an iron lever attached to the stones. He pulled it down.

There was a sudden clank, and a hidden door opened, leading into an underground passageway. The wizard placed his feet on the doorway and swung himself into the unlighted hallway.

The air was damp and stuffy, and the sound of his heavy breathing encircled him.

"Luxo!" he whispered, and a white light glowed from the tip of his wand, illuminating the narrow space. The thick scent of moist earth permeated the space, and spider webs blanketed the ceiling. He paced slowly on the damp stone floor as he recalled the better days of this underground place.

At last, Elmagos stood in front of a wooden door—the entrance to the old cellar. As he opened the door, he wondered if it too had stayed the same, or if something unforeseen awaited him inside. A candle flickered in the dark, revealing a man's shadowy face. Clouds of smoke came out of his pipe, and he looked like a ghost.

The man raised his head and cleared the fog with a trembling hand. He gaped at Elmagos standing in the doorway with his illuminated wand. For long moments, the two men stood as still as if they were rooted deep in a glacier.

"Blessed are the gods..." the wizard mumbled in disbelief.

"Elmagos..." The man jumped on his feet and found his tongue. "My dear friend, we meet again in the most unexpected place."

"You have made me believe in ghost tales!" Elmagos shook his head and rushed to him.

"Not just ghosts, but Sea Ghosts!" Robin hugged the cloaked man, and they burst into loud laughter.

The captain couldn't let go. "How can I ever thank you for raising my son all of those years..." he whispered.

The wizard nodded with a smile.

"What the devil are you doing here, Robin?"

"I was looking for you, Elmagos, and had to bring you some urgent news. The only man in the North I could trust was Romi. If you recall, we served together as captains in our early days. And so I headed to his inn. When I saw the many folks in front, I had no choice but to come here, to our secret place. Unfortunately, the old passage to the inn is barred." Robin pointed toward a thick oaken door that used to connect between the underground chamber and the cellars beneath the inn's kitchen.

Elmagos nodded and put his arm on Robin's shoulder. "We both carry much weight on our tongues, but before we start, let us make some order in this tedious place." He smiled and waved his wand.

The captain sat in silence as furniture floated in the air, candles lit, and the room was cleansed of dust and spiderwebs.

Elmagos crossed his arms, pleased. "Almost like the old days," he said, then they both slid into chairs at the table. "More than nine years have passed since our last meeting, and I have much to tell you."

"Indeed…" Robin puffed a long cloud. "I am sure you will find my story remarkable as well."

The wizard went first, informing the captain about the mysterious kidnappings all around Low Earth. Then he followed with the events in the White Castle, Zigler, and the magical visit to the Veerlands. When the wizard mentioned sailing with Mago, the captain had a broad smile on his face, but as soon as he told him about the dark conversation with the queen and the discovery of the Tree of Wands in the Cloak Castle, Quint's face turned white.

At last, the green-cloaked wizard concluded his story with his recent journey and findings at the Navy fortress. None of them spoke for long minutes after.

"I came here to evade Zigler's spies and speak with Romi," Elmagos broke the silence. "Instead, I found the best surprise I could ever dream of."

Nonetheless, Robin's face remained grim and stern. "It is far worse than I imagined." He shook his head. "Wait until you hear my tale."

He began by telling shortly about his adventures on the *Skulls Cleaver* with the crew and all of their remarkable discoveries. Then he told Elmagos all about the two suspicious Navy ships near the Southland and how they followed them to the North.

When the captain mentioned the Bloody Shirts, and Alec and Lia, the wizard's heart thundered. For the first time, he heard about the terrible event at the Four Miracles Castle. His legs swayed and bumped against the table. His mind wandered to the many poor orphans he knew, his friend Nestor, and all the rest of the teachers. With his eyes open, he could see them being brutally dragged from their beds by these vicious men. His hands clenched into mighty fists and he banged the table with fury.

"They will pay for their actions!" Elmagos snarled with blazing eyes.

The steam from the wizard's ears dissipated and Robin went on about Neal, Rollo's treasure, and Rusty's loss. When he mentioned Mago and Lallo sailing back from a secret island in the Treacherous Sea, the wizard leaned forward.

"Thanks to those two half-wits," Quint said, "we discovered the gap in the Frosty Reef. They also said you had arrived in the North, so I had to take the risk of coming here and inform you about everything that had happened."

Elmagos took a long puff. Of all the things Robin had told him, one was resonating in his head—the secret island. Question after question stirred his mind, and he became utterly consumed in the world between his ears.

Suddenly, the captain clasped his sword. His face froze as he signed the wizard to be silent, pointing at the locked door. They could hear voices behind it. Elmagos held his wand, and Robin's hand pressed against the hilt.

Zigler spies… Elmagos thought. He was prepared for anything. A moment later, a tall shadow slammed open the door and strode into the room.

"If I had known of your arrival ahead of time, I would have prepared a royal feast, my friends," a towering man spoke with an apologetic voice. When he swung his pumpkin head into the room, his legs went rigid, and he dropped a large basket of food on the floor.

"Wh…what…" Romi's lips seemed to be glued together. He couldn't utter a word as he stared at Elmagos and the captain.

"Come and say hello to your old friend," Robin called out to the innkeeper.

Then Laos the Orange and Petri the Blue stepped into the room, one behind the other, each one with his own puzzled face.

"How did…? When…? I can't believe it!" Excited calls and cheers filled the room, and they all surrounded the legendary Sea Ghost, not letting him breathe.

"My friends!" Elmagos chuckled. "There will be time for excitement later."

"How did you all know to meet here?" asked the captain, full of astonishment.

"The message Elmagos sent said to meet him at Romi's Inn and be secretive about it," Petri answered indifferently. "So we assumed that he meant the hidden underground cellar."

"We were sailing north and reached the harbor under the thick fog, not a half an hour ago," said Laos. "By that time, the tavern was closed, so we sneaked to the front. No one saw us."

Elmagos slumped in his seat with a troubled face. "Sit down, my friends," he said. "It's a long story, and you should pay attention to all the details. Perhaps you will find other meanings than I did."

The time was about midnight, and when Elmagos and Captain Robin finished their stories, dawn had come. Romi went back up to the inn and brought down more blankets and food. Soon they all fell asleep, for they were quite weary.

They didn't wake until noon, which was enough time for the wizards to digest the news. Laos of the East was the first to talk.

"I assume we all know by now that there is an island somewhere in the Treacherous Sea, and it would seem that the Bloody Shirts have brought all of their captives to this place. We also know—" He took a puff of his pipe. "—that based on Elmagos's discoveries, the Navy maintains a budget for about 200 ships. However, in truth, there are only fifty warships patrolling the ocean, and ten that are always docked in Crescent Harbor. A total of sixty ships!"

"The rest of the regions send resources every year to sustain 200 ships?" Petri shook his head. "How is it possible? Where are the remaining vessels?"

"After talking to Neal the Eel," Robin joined the conversation, "I know for a fact that the pirates have captured no more than twenty ships."

"That still leaves about 120 Navy warships unaccounted for," Elmagos interrupted. "And it is my guess that they are docked at the secret island where a new Navy base has been established."

The wizards exchanged glances, and the murmurs filled the room.

"My friends!" Elmagos spoke with a serious tone. "I am afraid someone had built a strong Army and Navy with the funds from our own lands and under our very long noses."

"Zigler!" Laos cried in anger. "We should bring this snake to justice at once!"

Petri nodded in agreement.

"No!" Elmagos shouted, and they all looked puzzled. Of all of them, the green cloak disliked the crown prince the most, yet now he seemed to protect him.

"Zigler plays a role, yes," Elmagos explained. "But we need him to lead us to the real culprit behind the plot."

Petri sounded much less convinced. "What makes you so sure it's not only Zigler's doing? We are all familiar with his devious character. In my opinion, he is fully capable of all these machinations."

"You forget the story of the boy, Kordos," said Elmagos. "The dragon rider who freed the Ravens from the Veerlands prison. There are seven of them, wizards and witches of the black cloaks, hiding on that same secret

Island. Who knows what they are plotting? No...no... Someone else is involved."

The appearance of Romi with baskets of roasted chicken sandwiches interrupted their discussion, and soon enough, the sounds of chewing took over.

"It's already twilight," the innkeeper said. "I brought three fresh horses to the back yard."

"What would we do without you, my dear friend?" Elmagos embraced the big man, and everyone thanked him again for his hospitality and friendship.

"Robin..." the wizard said. "Sail back to your ship and watch the path to the Treacherous Sea. I shall meet you again here, a week from today, just before the opening ceremony for the Wizards' Game."

The captain smiled at him and departed. As the three wizards were about to leave the room, Elmagos declared, "To the Cloak Castle, our old-new home!"

The weight and burden of the afternoon discussions left them at once, and a new hope filled their hearts.

CHAPTER 6

A SHORT REVELATION

Kordos remembered the moment when he stood motionless in Seros's room as the sound of Elmagos's footsteps grew fainter until he heard nothing at all. Grim loneliness captured his heart. He was left in the mysterious Cloak Castle all by himself—or even worse, in the company of the ghosts of slain children. That thought, and the odd noises during the night, kept him prisoner here.

For two days, he tiptoed around his room, cautious of making any sound—but he wasn't idle at all. Like a curious cat, he scanned Seros's books on the shelves. Most were complex and difficult to grasp. "The Rules for the Young Sorcerers" was quite boring, so he turned his eyes to "All About Wands" and "Basic Charms and Spells," which were even more tedious.

One particular shelf at the bottom, behind the desk, grabbed his attention. It was labeled on the side: "Wizardry for Beginners." When he opened the book, a parchment dropped out of the binding.

It read: "This is my greatest work in teaching magic to the novice wizard. Its revolutionary new methods will shorten the practice time tenfold."

To his utmost wonder, the drawings inside were actually *moving*. He read the instructions with an open mouth.

Each page taught a technique or a charm to perform magic. A wizardly figure would do or say something with a distinct tone, and the trainee had to drill and perfect it. Only when the apprentice produced an excellent result would he pass to the next lesson. The training was built in a step-by-step manner, and it allowed the trainee to proceed only if they perfected the levels before. The speed of learning depended entirely on the student and their hunger to study.

It turned out to be the most fascinating thing Kordos had ever learned, and before he knew it, the time was flying by.

From dawn till midnight Kordos practiced, performing elementary motions with a wooden stick in his room.

On the third day, he woke a few hours after daybreak. The sun flashed through the balcony's doors, and the sky was cloudless. He bounced from the bed as though he was late for an important meeting, but a moment later, he realized he had nowhere to go and nothing to hurry for.

Like each morning since Elmagos left, he stepped out to the sunny balcony, breathed the crisp northern air, and made himself breakfast.

The views around him were too striking to digest. He gulped his tea and gazed many miles ahead. The peaks of the Snowy Mountains speared a host of rainclouds drifting from the Wild Sea. On their ashen slopes, shimmering silver waterfalls cascaded to the rivers below.

Northeast of Norvita, the turfy plains mantled the earth, and his keen shepherd's eyes noted tiny white dots spreading on the vast green carpet.

"Sheep..."

A slight shiver ran through him, and he closed his eyes. His mind carried him all the way to the pastures of Thousand Knolls. As he was herding his flock, the morning dew wetted his feet, and the fresh scent of grass pervaded the air.

Suddenly, a strong wave of longing for his brothers and Ingram crashed against his chest. Goosebumps crawled on his skin as though he had dived into a freezing lake. He yearned to stroll on those grassy hills, but when he stared back at the room, he sighed.

Ghosts or not, he thought, *it's about time I get out of Seros's room.* Before he left, he gave one last glance toward the east, but his sharp eyes caught something that rooted him to the spot.

A thread of smoke was rising from the Giant Wand of the Cloak Castle. It came just at the point where the Wizard's Right Palm gripped the Wand. Kordos's heart rumbled, and cold sweat coated his body.

There is someone in the Cloak Castle... He shuddered. *But how is it possible? Elmagos said it has been blocked for seventy years.*

He searched hard for any movement but saw nothing. The Wand's base had a domed ceiling that hid anything inside.

Determined to solve this riddle, Kordos hurried inside, donned his clothes, and went out into the castle for the first time.

His days in the magically refreshed chamber had made him forget about the rest of the castle—dark, dusty, and filled with spiderwebs in every corner.

The suffocating air made his head spin. It was as though he was five stories underground and not in a towering statue hundreds of feet in the air.

Kordos rushed through the corridors in the dormitory, down the curved staircase, and crossed the great hall. A minute later, he descended the spiral steps of the Neck. Clear blue sky glimpsed at him through the elongated windows. At the bottom, he gave a slight push to the secret door. It opened soundlessly into the grand library.

At last, he took a deep breath. The gigantic, vaulted space was ventilated and bright due to the dozens of glass panels on each side of the Shoulders. He passed among many desks and crowded bookshelves until he reached the Right Shoulder. Through the dirty panes, he couldn't yet see the Wizard's Wand.

How can I reach the outside? There must be a way to get out there…

After minutes of grinding thoughts, his eyes fell on the floor and spotted a shaft of sunlight in the corner. A tall ladder was attached to the wall, leading up to a hatch in the high ceiling.

Like a cat, he hastened up the rungs. He threw the hatch open, and a strong gust of cold wind almost knocked him to the floor.

Although he was an outstanding climber and used to heights, it gave Kordos the shivers. He tried again with much more caution. His hands seized the edge as he clambered up.

A frigid wind dried the perspiration on his face as he kneeled on the Right Shoulder. He gripped the rough stone beneath him. *At least the surface isn't slippery…*

From his spot, his eyes followed a narrow path running down to the Arm and the Wrist. Above the Fingers that curled around the Wand, a terrace was covered by a domed ceiling, and a wisp of smoke continued to rise from underneath.

Kordos advanced low and slow between sky and earth, ready for any gust of wind that might sweep him into the air and cast him to his death. Fortunately, no gust came his way.

Winding stone stairs were carved into the Fist, leading to the top of the Thumb. There was no railing—this climb was certainly not for the faint of heart.

He placed his feet lightly on the crumbling stairs and prayed they could carry his weight. His heartbeat raced as he crept and watched the smoky clouds drifting through the morning sky. Soon, a sweet aroma mixed with the crisp air.

Five feet below the Wand's base, he halted, raised his head slightly above the floor, and saw what he couldn't see from Seros's balcony.

A round patio about twenty feet in diameter had six white marble columns supporting the domed roof. The columns had many cracks and grooves, as though they had been carved to resemble ancient oak trees. A fire pit stood in the center, surrounded by seats of stone. A sudden gurgling noise followed by coughing came to Kordos's ears, and his heart thundered.

He climbed another step and pushed his head higher, seeking out the source of the sound.

A short man garbed in brown was lying comfortably on a bench, reading a book. Smooth silver hair mantled his scalp and cheeks. Beside him lay a bottle and wooden staff.

Kordos watched him with stunned eyes as he sipped and gurgled wine in his mouth like a child. The man seemed calm, so Kordos decided to approach him. He stepped up and stood high on the patio.

"Good morning to you, sir…" he spoke softly, not wanting to scare the man.

But all the same, the book flew from the man's hand, and the bottle shattered on the floor. The little man's shocked hazel eyes gaped at the boy with such puzzlement and curiosity that it seemed as though he had never seen people before.

After a long, tense silence, he sat. The brown cloak covered his short legs, which couldn't reach the ground. He gazed at the spilled wine, then swift as an arrow, he bolted and stopped a foot away from the lad, measuring him with sharp eyes.

Kordos froze in utter astonishment, not daring to make a move. Never before had he seen someone move at such a speed. Not only that, Kordos could now see that he wasn't a man at all, but a dwarf. He barely reached Kordos's chest.

They looked at each other from up close, and the short one lowered his gaze and seemed quite embarrassed by his foolish reaction.

"Forgive me," he said with a surprisingly deep voice. "I didn't expect to see a live person here…"

"There is nothing to forgive, sir. My name is Kordos of the Southland." He bowed.

The dwarf smiled. "And I am Viggo of the Endless Forest, your hidden neighbor to the south."

"How did you get here?" they both asked at the same moment.

Viggo led him to sit on a bench. "Are you a young wizard, my boy?"

"Perhaps. A wizard's boy, nothing more." Kordos laughed. He noted a staff with a silver mouth shape at its top. *Is it possible the dwarf is a…?*

Viggo followed Kordos's gaze. "My story is long, but I promise to make it as short as myself." He gave a meaty chortle, then continued. "As I said before, my name is Viggo, and I am from the Gerfeelk clan. My people dwell in the southeast part of the Endless Forest, where the Sting Mountains cast their shadows over the mighty trees.

"For thousands of years my tribe has lived there, surviving challenges, wars, and enemies. Our race was entrusted with the sacred knowledge of healing and speaking the animals' tongues. With these gifts, we treat and heal all creatures in need.

"But then, not more than five weeks ago, my people faced a threat like no other. When one of my kin went to cure a badly wounded wild man in the forest, he caught a rare disease that we had never encountered before. Soon enough, many of our people grew ill and were dying.

"My father, who is also the tribe's leader, and a few of the elders searched for every medicine and treatment. However, nothing stopped the sickness. Some days later, Seros the Indigo appeared in our land."

Kordos's eyes opened wide, and his heart froze as he recalled Elmagos's tale about the academy's massacre. "Is Seros alive? Is he in the Endless Forest?"

Viggo measured the boy with an astonished expression. "Do you know him?"

"Only heard of him from Elmagos, the green wizard. It would gladden him to know his friend is alive and well."

The dwarf sighed. "Alive he is, but not so well. His face is grim and gloomy, and I need to reckon hard to remember him smiling. The poor man chose a life of isolation, but nonetheless, no one can question his brilliance and knowledge. Seros was the only one to recognize the source of this rare disease. It came from an animal in the Werewolf Forest."

"The Werewolf Forest?" Kordos stuttered. "But that's all the way here, in the far North. How did it get to the Endless Forest in the South?"

"That was the exact question we asked ourselves," replied Viggo. "Nevertheless, no one had an answer. Only guesses. Then Seros spoke about a plant called Lagalen, which grows in the Northern Kingdom and nowhere else. He said it can heal the wounded and stop the deadly plague. Unfortunately, he didn't recall where exactly it grew, but he did tell me there were many books of healing in the Cloak Castle of Norvita. He promised that one must contain the information I need.

"Next, he explained of the safest route to the North and the secret tunnel into the abandoned castle. There was no time to waste, so I volunteered for the task. It was a monumental risk, for my people have never traversed Low Earth and had no business with its people. In fact, except for a few incidents, men from your regions have never seen dwarves.

"And so I went on my journey, running day and night toward Norvita. Through harsh wilderness I traveled, for I picked an obscure path along the jagged ridges of the Range of Heroes. Many animal friends assisted me along the way—some bore me on their backs, and others brought guidance and food. Yet, some wild beasts hunted me, and I barely escaped with my life.

"Finally, I sneaked to Norvita at night, went through the underground tunnel, and emerged here in the castle. For two weeks I have been reviewing the numerous volumes, but I have found no mention of that plant yet. I pray with all my heart not to be late."

The dwarf ended with a deep sigh. He grabbed his pipe and puffed some white smoke.

Kordos sat dumbfounded on his chair, digesting this remarkable story. "How old are you?" he asked with a puzzled voice.

"I am eighty years old. My kin were blessed with long life, and like our ancestors, some of us reach 300 years. But enough about me and my sad venture, for it brings only sorrow to the heart. Let's hear your tale, my lad, and fill an old soul with hope," said Viggo with glinting eyes.

Kordos hesitated, for he recalled Elmagos warning that no one should know that he was in the castle.

But then, the dwarf already knew much about Seros and the wizards. There was something about his genuine tone and mannerisms that made Kordos feel at ease with this short stranger. He didn't trust him fully, but before long, Kordos found himself telling the dwarf all about his shepherd's life and spoke briefly about the journey north and their breakfast with the queen in the Crown Garden. However, he mentioned nothing about the Floating Islands, the dragon, or the Tree of Wands. He said that the main reason Elmagos entered the Cloak Castle was to hide from curious eyes.

Suddenly Viggo gave him a cold stare. "Swear you won't tell him anything about me."

"Why?" Kordos asked in surprise. "You should not fear him or the wizards. They are all honorable men."

"I am sure they are, but it's not that," Viggo said with a genuine voice. "They will start questioning me about Seros and many other events in the Endless Forest. We dwarves are healers and are very careful not to be involved in matters of politics—or wars. I just want to get the cure and leave!"

The boy nodded and decided not to add more distress to the situation. "As you wish, sir! Now that we are here in this castle together, I will help you in any way I can to find the information you seek."

"Gratitude, my lad! Now follow me to the library if you can," he said as he took his staff and zoomed out of the terrace.

Kordos rushed behind him, but the dwarf sped down the crumbling stairs like a rabbit. By the time Kordos had reached the Hand, Viggo had already vanished into the hatch like a mouse. He had no chance to match his lightning speed, so he moved slowly across the open space and tried not to fall.

***

After many hours of scanning and searching through the ocean of volumes in the library, the two slumped on the floor.

"I want you to teach me about magic," said Kordos out of the blue.

Viggo studied him from head to toe, as though he was examining an item in a store.

"Magic is more complicated than you think… It can cost you dearly if you falter."

"I promise to put all my heart and mind into it," pleaded the boy.

"It's too risky…"

"Elmagos trusted me with high secrecy; does that not count?"

Viggo's eyes inspected him again and seemed to reconsider. "The great wizard, you say?" He pursed his lips. "Well, if Elmagos trusts you, then perhaps so should I…"

"Thank you, master!" Kordos's heart thumped with excitement.

"No need for such etiquette, my lad! I am just a humble dwarf."

With that said, both needed a break from the tedious work and headed to Seros's room.

"You already used some magic here," Viggo said as they entered, clearly quite impressed. "Are you certain you need me at all?"

"Elmagos did it. I just watched."

The next days went by slowly for the novice wizard and his teacher, although Kordos was advancing swiftly through the beginner's magic book. When Viggo needed some escape from the constant search in the library, he honed the boy's techniques and guided him with much patience and wisdom.

With every passing moment, Kordos realized how fortunate he was to have the dwarf master by his side. Tough and demanding but also wise and brilliant, Viggo thrust him to the edge, forcing him to find his powers one after the other.

Soon enough, the turning pages grew thick, and the bond between the two even thicker, as they shared moments of success and frustration.

In just one week, Kordos had finished the first book and, ten days later, he had also completed a book called "Second Grade Wizardry." By then, Viggo announced that he had an exceptional young man on his hands.

A day after, he burst into Seros's room.

"I found it my lad! At last!"

The dwarf kissed the book in his hands, and a triumphant smile curled on his face.

Kordos hurried to his friend and embraced him. "I am so glad, Viggo! You are the hero of the Endless Forest."

"Seros is my hero," he said swiftly. "This book has a map and all the knowledge I need. Now I must leave; I cannot linger." He opened his pack, shoved the volume inside, and swung it onto his back.

Then his hazel eyes landed on the boy. "Your progress has been remarkable and swift until now. Let's see if you can keep this pace with more challenging study." He dashed to the shelf and tossed him "Skills for the Intermediate Wizard."

"Until our next meeting, Kordos, son of Dancing Bow..." said the dwarf. As he rushed out the door, men's voices came from the chambers below.

CHAPTER 7

THE DRUNKEN MAIDEN

"Ouch!" Lia hissed painfully as she pulled her squashed hand from under Alec's foot, giving him a nasty glance.

"Shhhhhh!" he snapped at her. "They might hear you."

A moment later, he realized he had stepped on her gentle fingers with the full weight of his body.

"Sorry." He took her hand swiftly and rubbed it with his fingers. At once, her eyes softened.

For the last two days, they had been hiding behind barrels, boxes, and old blankets in the hold of the *Drunken Maiden*.

While Mago was snoring or yelling at poor Lallo, they were sitting quietly beside each other and eating their stolen food.

It was only last night when Captain Quint had left for Crescent Harbor.

"Mago! I am leaving now and will be back tomorrow night," they heard him saying in a cold voice.

"Good luck, Captain, and be safe!" Lallo called from the mast. "We will be waiting for you right here."

"We won't move until you return, Captain!" Mago said with a note of importance in his voice, making sure he was the one to speak last.

During the day, the two birdbrains went to the harbor's market and bars, while the two Eagles left their hidden nest and had the place to themselves.

At last, they could stretch their bones and found all sorts of tasty fruit and bread under Mago's bed, keeping it out of Lallo's sight.

Sunset arrived, and Lia caught a glimpse of the two wobbling happily on the pier. The bottles of rum swayed in their hands, and they seemed light and empty.

These are not their first bottles today; she thought as their silly singing came closer. *I hope the fools kept their mouths shut about Robin's visit.* The time had come for the two youngsters to get back behind the wine barrels below deck. Mago and Lallo climbed aboard and continued to revel as the sun sank in the west.

The night darkened, and a figure crept aboard.

"Mago..." Robin whispered into the dark. "Prepare the ship; we go back."

"Aye, aye, Captain Qui—" Mago shouted, but Quint smacked his mouth.

"Listen to me, you drunken pig!" he growled at him with lightning eyes and clutched Mago's throat.

"Argh...awk...arrrgh..." was all Mago could reply.

"If you speak my name again, I will feed you to the sharks. Now move and set sail!" Robin shoved him backward.

Mago's face turned pale as the moon above. He rushed to the mast and pulled ropes and opened sails, shouting commands to Lallo the whole time.

Minutes later, they departed the Crescent Harbor, sailing toward the west and the *Cleaver*.

In the dark, lurking, the Eagles were following each gesture on Robin's face. His fingers scratched his scalp slowly, and his thin wrinkles seemed to have grown deeper. The gaze on his face became distant.

"I wonder what news he received…" Lia murmured with concern.

"I have the impression it was not encouraging," Alec murmured.

"Poor Robin. Too much lays on his shoulders. He won't think bad of us, will he, Alec?" Guilt and panic crammed her voice. A silence followed as the boy eyed the troubled captain.

"We owe it to our brothers and sisters! They must have been tortured by now on Death Island. We must help them in any way we can!" he said with a determined look.

Goosebumps crawled on Lia's skin, filling her with confidence. Never before had she recognized Alec's spark and strength, but now, a fire blazed in him. Her racing heart was melting like butter on a sunny day, realizing she was falling in love with this new Alec.

The *Drunken Maiden* sailed all night long and was kept surprisingly sturdy by her two drunk, frightened sailors.

Late the next morning, they spotted the *Skulls Cleaver.* It looked like any other Navy ship, except for the white sail that masked the figurehead on the bowsprit.

The *Drunken Maiden* approached the hull, and Robin shook both Mago's and Lallo's hands and scanned their faces.

"Thank you for taking me to the harbor."

"A great honor!" Lallo answered genuinely and bowed.

"Good luck, Captain…" Mago said shortly. He seemed anxious for the moment he would be the only master on board.

"Remember," Robin called behind him as he climbed the rope, "not a word!"

"Aye, aye, Captain Qui—" Lallo bellowed and Mago slapped his head. Quint gave him a final harsh glare and disappeared on his ship.

***

"Welcome back, Captain!" Mello said, but he didn't have the usual grin on his face.

"What is it?" Robin halted as he watched his man shifting nervously, avoiding his gaze. At last, his disappointed eyes faced his master.

"Neal and Pozzo are gone!"

"What do you mean gone?"

"They disappeared! Vanished from the ship, and with them Alec and Lia!" Resentment filled Mello's voice.

The captain stood silent and shook his head in disbelief.

"But why?" he mumbled as he stared blankly into space. "We treated them like brothers…"

"They all planned it together. They took one of the skiffs on the night you left. We should have never believed them!" the Sea Ghost snarled.

A sheen covered Robin's heated forehead. "I trusted them all, and instead they repay us with treachery?" Suddenly, his eyes opened wide, and he bolted to his cabin. The shelf where he had placed Rollo's map and necklace now stood empty.

Mello, who dashed behind his captain, froze at the door just in time to witness Robin furious like never before.

The usually composed captain blew steam from his nostrils, and his eyes flared, scorching his face like a glowing ember.

In a blink of an eye, he slammed the wooden desk with his mighty fists, and the deep boom filled the room.

Then, he gave a stormy cry that shook the entire sea.

"Neallllllllllll!"

CHAPTER 8

CAPTAIN EEL

"Haaa!" Neal woke up at once from his light nap.

"What happened, Captain Eel?" Pozzo stared at his friend, wiping the sweat from his forehead.

"Did you hear that?" he asked with an odd expression on his face.

Pozzo looked around. "Hear what? It's only us here…" He gave Neal a concerned glance and handed him some water. "Perhaps it's the heat, Captain. I myself am drenched in sweat."

"Perhaps you are right, shipmate…" He gulped and sighed, feeling much more refreshed.

For the last two days, their boat and its little sail bore them briskly on the calm sea. Neal navigated them skillfully, following the stars—and his new map. The further southwest they sailed, the warmer it had become.

"We are not far from the Bone Isles!" Neal announced on the third night while perspiration dripped down his face.

"How do you know, Captain?" Pozzo asked, baffled. During the day, they had seen nothing but the infinite blue ocean, and now it was dark all around them.

"Use your mind, shipmate, not your blind eyes!" the Eel snapped cleverly. "Don't you feel the muggy weather, the change in the air?"

A broad grin spread on Pozzo's face. "I almost forgot about the stinky bastards, sweating at all times."

The Bone Isles that Neal referred to—or the Pirates' Islands, as many people called them—were a group of hundreds of Islands, scattered between the Sapphire and the Misty Seas. Some were tiny and had only a few structures, while others were as large as the greatest cities in Low Earth.

The strangest mixture of people inhabited these isles, and among them were the Sea Bastards, fugitives, and wanted criminals.

However, the majority of the people were the indigenous islanders and ordinary folks who had left Low Earth in search of better opportunities. Oddly enough, they all lived relatively in peace. Dwelling in these exotic paradises, each followed his own beliefs, culture, and rules.

Long, magnificent reefs and sandbars surrounded most of the islands, serving as the best possible defense against the mighty Navy warships. Only a few skilled master seamen such as Rollo and Neal could navigate a three-master through these tricky conditions, and most were pirates. The Navy captains dared not to risk such a task, and the few who attempted were buried with their vessels. Nonetheless, many of the larger islands were surrounded by deep water and were much more susceptible to sudden attacks from the Royal Fleet.

At dawn, the sea was smooth as glass and the sky turned silver-blue, free of clouds and mist.

Neal jumped on his feet and rocked the little skiff. Pozzo, whose heavy snoring could have disturbed the giant whales in the deep, didn't move.

"Wake up, shipmate!" He kicked his friend with excitement and pointed to the horizon. "An island!"

Pozzo sat up and rubbed his eyes. The blur turned clear, and a distant land came into sight.

"You did it, Captain!" He gazed at his idol with awe.

"I couldn't have done it without my first mate!"

Neal cheered, and the two burst into laughter. He was now light as a feather, and all of his concerns about navigating the vulnerable skiff in the vast ocean faded away. For long minutes, the Eel explained to Pozzo what they were about to do and showed the route on his chart.

Occupied with their plans, they missed something to the south. When Neal raised his eyes off the map, his heart stopped. A ship had been sailing toward their boat, blocking them from reaching the island ahead.

Neal knew it had spotted them with ease on the unruffled sea. No place to hide, no chance to escape. He grabbed his face with frustrated hands.

"Why? Why? Why?" He groaned. Unbearable thoughts of becoming a prisoner again tortured his mind.

Pozzo stared at the approaching vessel in panic and mumbled prayers to all the gods he knew.

"So close..." the Eel grunted as he eyed the island behind the ship. "Over my dead body will you get Rollo's treasure!" he hissed.

He rotated the heel of his boot, and it opened with a click. Then he folded down the map as much as he could and pressed it inside, turning the sole back to its original position. He put Rollo's necklace around his neck.

Moments later, sailors in red shirts appeared on the approaching ship, and Pozzo's trembling feet shook the skiff.

"Captain..." His voice broke. "If one of the Bloody Shirts recognizes me, they will hang me for desertion. Once you join them, there is no way back, except death!"

"Let's hope this is not the same ship you served on," Neal said with a quiet voice. "When they ask, we will say that we are simple folks from one of the islands.

It wasn't long before the ship pulled alongside and dropped a ladder down to their little boat.

"Bring them up and put them with the rest of the prisoners!" an officer barked.

Neal and Pozzo surrendered without a fight, and the guards tied them swiftly and dragged them below deck.

Pozzo breathed a sigh of relief. No one paid any particular attention to them. They seemed safe now, surrounded by many captives in the dark.

Under the dim lantern light, Neal scanned the folks around him and his heart boomed. Puzzled and terrified faces of the natives crowded the gloomy space.

These cruel bastards have reached the larger islands, thought the Eel. *Soon, there won't be any safe place.*

"To Vermilion Island!" came the officer's voice again, reminding both of the awaiting hell.

CHAPTER 9

THE EAGLES' SHIELD

The *Drunken Maiden* was also sailing to the Vermilion Island, the Bloody Shirts' hidden base beyond the Frosty Reef. It carried a precious load of fine wine barrels and a hidden nest with two lovebirds. Throughout the voyage, the youngsters found themselves in each other arms, kissing.

After dropping Robin at the *Skulls Cleaver,* life turned back to normal as Mago drained bottles of rum and barked commands at Lallo. Under his captain's probing eyes, the poor sailor was running like a fearful rabbit from mast to sail to the wheel.

At last, they reached the passage and dropped anchor until a small rowboat with a lantern guided them across the Frosty Reef. Beyond that, the smugglers navigated with skill and caution into the dark.

They had traveled this route dozens of times, yet their hearts raced each and every voyage. One blunder, and none of them would live to see the sunrise.

Alec and Lia glimpsed from the porthole below deck, staring as they sailed along icebergs.

Lia's hazel eyes widened. "How is this drunk captain able to do it?"

"Let's prepare ourselves before they dock in the harbor," said Alec beside her.

While Mago and Lallo navigated on deck, the boy scanned for anything that might help them slip away unseen. He found a rope and tied it to the window at the stern. Lia gave him a puzzled glance.

"When we reach the pier, we must climb down swiftly and swim to shore," Alec said.

"The water must be freezing here!" Lia's voice was discontent.

"We have no other choice, unless you can come up with a better idea."

She gazed at him with a silent tongue.

"I will warm you up later. I promise." He gave her a playful kiss, and the red-haired fox smiled.

"Lallo!" Mago suddenly called from above. "This time we anchor at the little dock on the northern part of the island."

"Aye, aye, Captain!" a faint voice answered high on the mast.

Alec and Lia peered from the porthole toward the west; they were sailing along a great harbor with many Navy ships. The busy dock swarmed with Bloody Shirts loading and unloading cargo by torchlight. When they noticed the *Drunken Maiden* passing by, some of them whistled and seemed very excited about the new delivery.

Alec's voice trembled. "I am glad we aren't stopping here…"

"Let's hope the other pier is not as crowded," Lia agreed, gaping at the dozens of vessels nearby. A half an hour later, their boat began slowing down.

"Prepare to dock!" Mago shouted. The two Eagles noted that they were headed for a small dock lit by a few dim lanterns.

Only two Navy ships and a few rowboats were moored here, while bored watchmen were standing on the pier. They stared at the *Drunken Maiden* with indifference.

Alec rushed to the back window.

"Let's go!" he said, helping her climb out first.

She lowered herself without a noise, gripping the rope tight. Just as she met the icy water, he untied it and slid down after her.

For a few moments they floated in the dark water, and puffs of steam came from their mouths as they both breathed and shivered. The piercing water froze their lungs, and each breath felt like a lump of ice traveling through their throat. Alec knew they might die in a matter of minutes.

"Li… Li… Lia." His voice was quivering, and his lips became numb. "Foll… Follow…me."

Lia couldn't speak. She just nodded her head like a mad woodpecker.

He clasped her hand, and they swam under the surface with only their eyes and noses sticking out.

Seconds later, they swam underneath the wooden dock. Alec made his way through the pylons until the sounds of steps and squeaking boards came over their heads. They halted at once, afraid of making the slightest noise. A guard was standing above them, refusing to move.

The freezing water stabbed their bodies like blades of ice. Alec glanced at Lia's face and knew she was beginning to lose control. Her body shivered violently, and her face turned white as snow.

He held her tight, rubbing her back with his hands as her chattery teeth nibbled on his neck.

Every moment seemed like an eternity, and the sentinel stood still above them. Alec couldn't wait a moment longer.

He carried Lia to a pylon and supported her hands on it. With a swift motion, he dived and seized a rock with his hand. Then he swam out from under the pier, and his eyes caught a glimpse of the shadow standing with his back toward him.

At once, he threw the rock high in the air. It fell on the other pier with a bang and splashed into the water. The bored watchmen turned their baffled faces to the sound and hurried toward it, leaving a clear path to the forest behind the dock.

With his last strength, Alec pulled Lia from the water and dragged her numb body toward the trees. They crawled on the mud and collapsed.

Her legs had turned into ice pillars and couldn't support her weight. She mumbled and shuddered at the same time.

"Stay here…" he said and covered her cold body with ferns. He saw a dim light ahead, and he moved that way. There, he found a small cabin among the trees.

Alec peered through the window. No one was inside, yet logs burned in a fireplace. He smelled the chimney smoke like it was a sweet bouquet of spring flowers—the fire gave him hope that they might survive.

Lia seemed a bit better when he returned, yet she continued to shiver. He placed her arms around his shoulders and led her back to the shack. They entered through the door, and a cozy heat welcomed their numbed bones.

A fire was burning on their left, and on the opposite wall stood a bed.

"Take off your clothes!" Alec snapped, and Lia stared at him with an open mouth.

"I promise I won't look." He smiled and grabbed a few blankets. He handed her one, gazing the other way while she wrapped herself with it. When she finished, he did the same, covering his body like an old mummy.

They put their wet clothes on the hearth as Alec peered outside through a crack in the door, making sure no shadows were coming their way.

In the meantime, Lia started coming back to herself. She paced around the little room, stretching her poor, trembling legs. At last, she sat beside the fireplace, gazed at the red flame, and dozed.

***

An hour later, Alec woke her with a cry.

"On your feet! A guard is coming!"

Alec shook her and quickly gathered their dry clothes. He thought about the window, but they couldn't make it on time. Their last resort was to hide.

A tall man opened the door, dropped his bow, quiver, and sword on the floor, and trudged to the bed. After muttering a few words, he sank on the mattress like a heavy rock, and before long, his snoring filled the shack.

Trapped underneath were the two Eagles. They dared not move or breathe.

Alec watched the burning logs and smiled to himself. His most intimate moments with Lia occurred under very strange circumstances—kissing back at Mago's boat, squeezing tight in the freezing water, and right here, under a Bloody Shirt's bed, blankets covering their naked bodies as they cuddled.

Soon enough, they fell asleep until the squeaking bed woke them up. The guard's boots banged the floor in front of them, and Lia clenched Alec's hand.

The man stood up, took up his weapons, and left the cabin, letting the cold wind slide in.

"We must leave before another one comes!" Alec insisted, pushing her out of their hiding place.

They put on their dry clothes and leather packs and searched the shack for anything that might help them survive the wilderness.

An old wardrobe in the corner of the room had everything they needed: bows, knives, and arrows, all laid carelessly around. They gathered weapons for themselves, and then in the small kitchen, they took a few bread loaves, some dried fruits, and smoked meat. Once they were equipped, they headed for the door. A peek through the crack revealed a dark night. There was no one close.

"Come on," Alec said, and they sneaked out to the forest.

The boy led the way toward the west, away from the harbor. Tall cedar trees surrounded them as they traveled deep into the unfamiliar terrain.

The further they went uphill, the more boulders were scattered on the dark ground. An hour later, they halted and laid flat on the cold soil as a wolf's howl pierced the night.

Alec crawled slowly and Lia beside him. They hid behind a mound of rocks, mantled with moss and ferns, and looked for the animal that made that sound. The two found no wolf, but something much larger.

A timber palisade, about thirty feet high and spread from south to north, blocked their path.

"Perhaps they keep the prisoners here," Lia whispered.

"But where are the guards?" Alec scanned around with puzzled eyes. "Let's try to find a way inside!" He stood up and marched north through the trees, searching for a gap in the wall without success.

A half a mile after, they came across a wide path in the forest. It started at the pier downhill and ended at a wooden gate in the palisade. To their utmost surprise, it was open, and the woods continued behind the mighty wall.

"I don't understand..." Lia murmured. "Why aren't they guarding it?"

"We have no choice but to keep forward," Alec said, but his voice was far from certain.

The two crept among the trees and opened their ears to any sound. But nothing came except howls and the chirps of crickets.

"Wait for my sign!" he said as they reached the last of the cedars before the wall. A moment later, he bolted to the gate, raced through it, and stopped at the first shadows beyond the wall.

A faint whistle followed, and Lia raced to join him. They kneeled beside each other and studied the darkness. All seemed quiet.

"A timber fence…an open gate…I can't figure it out," Alec said with frustration.

"It could be an old camp…" she half-mumbled.

With no answer for this riddle, they strode toward the west and hoped to find some hints ahead. The sea of pines enclosed them while a sudden mist crept from the east and filled the forest with an ashen blanket. Soon enough, Lia found no stars above, and Alec couldn't make his way.

"We should stay here until morning," he said. "The fog should burn off by then."

"I am fine with that," she said as she slumped to the ground amid the rocks and ferns.

The boy smiled and dropped his pack. A moment later, they cuddled underneath a blanket. The foggy night spread around and wetted their heads, but the two cared not and fell asleep.

***

Aowwww!

The sound of horns shattered the silence of the forest.

Aowwww!

A second wave followed, and both jumped into the air like frightened cats.

A cold dawn had arrived, and only scattered wisps of mist remained from the night before.

Lia's hair stood up on her arms.

"What are those sounds?"

Alec said nothing, but his jaw tensed.

They started moving when they heard screams from the east. The two exchanged a terrified glance and leaped behind a tree trunk. At once, they drew their bows and aimed toward the sounds. Sweat covered their faces as the wild screams grew closer.

"Ready…" Alec's voice trembled as the first man appeared. Next, nine more followed, speeding through the trees like a bunch of boars.

"Thirty yards…twenty…fifteen!" he counted.

Lia's heart thundered. She was about to release an arrow on a man when she froze and leaped out of her hiding place.

"Don't shoot, Alec!" she cried.

The terrified runners froze as soon as they saw Lia and Alec.

"Please...don't kill us!" a boy pleaded and burst into tears.

"Lower your bow!" she hissed at Alec.

There were ten of them. A few of them looked like pirates, and the rest were youngsters. One had a familiar face.

"Alec! Lia!" he cried in disbelief and hastened toward them, hugging both with all his might. His name was Albin. He was a thirteen-year-old orphan from the Four Miracles Castle.

The others stepped closer and huddled around them, gaping at the two Eagles fully armed with knives and bows.

"Albin!" she said. "What is this place? Where are our brothers and sisters from the shelter?"

"They are in the other part of the island," the boy explained with sad eyes. "Some are used as slaves, but others are warriors who are trained to fight in the arena. Every week the guards pull ten of us slaves from the mines for what they call the Hunting. Only a few return alive—and sometimes none."

"What do you mean, Albin?" Alec's voice shook.

"He meant exactly what he said!" one of the pirates snapped impatiently. "It's a hunting game for them, but death for us. The Bloody Shirts scatter us in this fenced forest. We have no way to escape and no weapons to protect ourselves. Our only option is to hide and run.

"Once we are let loose, the cruel bastards come into the confined area. Four men, armed with bows and arrows, swords, and knives. A few even carry spears. Then they start hunting, killing us for entertainment and coins."

"What… What are you saying?" Lia's eyes popped.

"Yes, maiden, you heard me right," the man said coldly. "It is a betting sport for them. Our lives mean nothing! Like any other thing on this island of death, people bet their fortune and coin on these games. Who killed the most? How many died? Who survived? It's all just a sick sport to these bloody bastards! The Bloody Shirts call this Vermilion Island, but we all call it Death Island. None of us will live to see our homes again."

Alec stared at them all. The ragged clothes couldn't conceal their beaten flesh and starving bones. The hate he felt for the Bloody Shirts burned his chest.

"I only wish one thing before death takes me..." said the pirate with a low voice. "That I will have the strength to tear one of these hunters to pieces."

They all cheered with vengeance cries and blazing eyes.

Aowwww!

The horns blew again and the cheering stopped. A terrible fear took over the revenge, and the shudders gripped their bones. They exchanged helpless glances with each other and prepared to flee to all directions.

"Wait!" Alec called furiously. "Unless you seek to die one by one, the only chance we have is working together!"

At once, he drew something on the ground, and they all gathered around him. The boy explained his simple strategy in a matter of seconds.

"Remember to work as one and bring them here. Today we will hunt them for a change!" he spat with vengeance.

In less than a minute, they all dispersed around the area, taking cover behind bushes and rocks.

Alec grabbed a rope from his pack and threw it on a high branch. Then, he and Lia clambered up and took positions, each facing a different direction with an arrow at the ready.

Many nerve-racking moments passed until an armed man appeared far to their right. He was moving slowly, searching the earth for tracks.

A stone was thrown at him from the trees and hit his back. He cursed and marched toward the ferns where it had come from, just near the tree where the Eagles were perched.

It was Lia's side, and the hunter crept with his bow, ready for his first kill. High up in the cedar, Lia held her bowstring tight, but the sweat was dripping on her shooting hand, making it tremble.

"He is about to butcher an innocent man," Alec whispered to her coldly. The sound of his words sent lightning into her hands. There was a *swoosh,* and an arrow pierced the hunter's chest. The man fell on his knees and glanced up, astonished, watching two Eagles protecting their young ones below.

Before he managed to cry, a rock crushed his skull. Two figures sprang out of their hiding places, dragged his body to a bush, and stripped him of his weapons.

Not a minute passed, and Alec spotted another hunter tiptoeing behind Albin. The boy hid behind a boulder and didn't see him. Tree branches stood in Alec's way, and he couldn't shoot from his spot. His heart was booming as he helplessly watched the hunter sneaking behind his young game.

With a swift decision, he tossed a stone at the pirate underneath him, signing with his trembling fingers to go and help Albin.

The pirate, who had taken the spear from the dead hunter, moved stealthily toward the killer. He found him drawing his bow with a smile and ready to shoot the boy in the back. He gave a mighty heave, and the spear skewered the hunter's ribs. The enemy dropped on his face.

Albin fell to his knees and sobbed as the pirate stripped the corpse of his weapons.

For a long hour, nothing happened. But no one left their positions.

When Alec signaled that a hunter was coming between them, they were ready for him. Three slaves jumped from the bushes and silently killed him with daggers.

It was a harsh scene. Alec watched high from the crown with stunned eyes. Utterly mesmerized by what had happened, he missed the last enemy. It was too late. The man seized a shaking boy and pressed a dagger against his throat.

"You'd better come out where I can see you, you little rats!" he cried, his head searching around him.

Alec couldn't shoot at the man's body, for he feared he'd also hit the victim. So he aimed at the hunter's head and prayed that the practice he had with the Rangers would pay off.

As the man laughed cruelly, a deadly arrow pierced through his neck. Two hours had passed since the hunt began, and the four hunters would hunt no more.

The two Eagles descended from their nest as everyone else emerged from behind bushes and rocks. They smiled at each other in relief.

"We owe you our lives!" the pirate said respectfully as everyone rallied under the protectors' tree. "Perhaps the next ones would think twice before they hunt us again."

They all cheered while Lia handed out pieces of bread and meat.

Later, the two Eagles learned that according to the hunt rules, the ones to survive were safe and not to be harmed, even if they managed to kill the hunters.

The day passed, and the slaves shared their horrible experiences. When Lia and Alec were asked how they escaped from the Bloody Shirts' ship, they said nothing about the *Skulls Cleaver*. Instead, Lia made up a story about a fishing boat that helped them out.

"The guards will be furious to find all of us alive, and the hunters all dead," one of the pirates said to Alec. "No one has ever killed this many hunters. Even with the rules, I am certain they will punish us for that later."

Lia caught a glimpse through the holes in his shirt, and her spine shuddered. Deep burn cuts spread on his back as though someone had carved his flesh with a red-hot blade.

"What if we all try to escape over walls?" She suggested.

"No, it won't work!" the pirate dismissed at once. "At dusk, the Bloody Shirts will search the entire area and butcher anyone trying to hide. But when we all show ourselves, they will search only for the dead hunters. No one knows the two of you are here, and you can leave again at dawn."

The scarred pirate stood.

"One last thing before we forget," he said. "You should take your arrows back, so it will seem that we used their weapons against them."

Lia and Alec exchanged a disgusted glance. They didn't want to deal with the corpses.

The pirate laughed. "Now you're squeamish? Don't worry, I will do it for you to return the favor."

With that said, he went to the bodies and yanked the arrows with much effort. "These damn youngsters know how to shoot!" he complained.

***

An hour later, Alec and Lia departed from the survivors and ascended a tree to wait out the night. A golden sunset painted the western sky, without a single drop of scarlet. Thanks to the young Eagles, much blood had been saved that day.

The horns sounded at twilight, signaling the end of the hunt. Fifteen minutes later, dozens of torches were heading toward them, and when the lights arrived, the ten survivors stood waiting.

The Bloody Shirts swarmed with barking hounds. They sniffed all around the trees and found the dead hunters in no time. They stared at the corpses in utter shock. They yelled and shouted and whipped the slaves, but nothing more.

As the Bloody Shirts marched back, two of their dogs yapped and scratched the trunk of a tree, refusing to obey their masters' commands. Two men came by and surveyed the tree's boughs with their torches.

On a high branch, Alec and Lia dripped sweat and prayed to the twilight stars for some luck.

"It might be a bear," a voice suggested.

"I've never eaten a roasted bear before." His friend laughed and placed a torch on the bark. In a few moments, the trunk turned into a giant flare.

The Bloody Shirts left the blazing tree behind and lashed the ten survivors all the way back to the gate.

CHAPTER 10

EVERYTHING ON THE LINE

The teams tossed a coin, and theirs was the first to choose. Edelin selected the first competition—shooting with stability. They placed a rope as thick as three fingers between two tree trunks, and one candidate from either squad took turns standing on it.

Each had a bow with five arrows and five knives. A round plate was situated thirty feet ahead. The animated crowd clustered behind the princess, who started first.

She walked slowly to the center of the rope, facing the mark. With exceptional focus, she shot the arrows and flung the knives while keeping herself steady on the shaky line.

When she came down, four arrows and three knives had pierced the target. Seven hits altogether.

"Well done, princess!" Niro yelled with pride, and both he and Tashunko hugged her warmly.

Jeffry's team sent their champion, and he stepped on the wobbly rope. He was slender and athletic and hit four arrows before he almost fell. Nevertheless, he regained his balance and stood back upright again, sticking four more knives into the target. A total of eight out of ten.

"One-nothing to Jeffry's team!" a young master announced, and the boys cheered.

Edelin stared at the ground. Fear and doubt conquered her mind. *They are better than us and might win the bet,* she thought in panic.

The boys' faces beamed with confidence as they selected the second game, a contest of speed and strength.

One candidate from each team had to run a hundred yards, pick up a heavy barrel on their back, and return to the starting line, where the next teammate would start their turn. The first group to carry three barrels across the finish line would be victorious.

Niro watched the princess, who turned pale like the moon. They all knew she was fast but not as strong as her companions.

"Edelin!" he whispered. "Tashunko and I will put all of our effort to give you an advantage on their third contender. "You will run last."

She nodded anxiously.

"Begin!" the master shouted, and everyone applauded as Niro and the slender boy raced side by side.

Niro reached his barrel first, picked it up on his shoulders, and sprinted back. When he passed the line, his opponent trailed fifteen yards behind him.

Tashunko bolted like a hound and opened up an even larger gap between him and the second contestant. The Black Tongue completed his task while the boy lagged twenty-five yards behind him.

"Go, Edelin, go!" the girls yelled, and she charged with all the speed she could muster. However, behind her ran none other than Jeffry. His legs galloped like a racing horse, closing the wide gap.

She picked up the last barrel and headed back to the starting line. The heavy weight squashed her graceful posture, but she still hurried and gasped like a miserable donkey.

Forty yards from the finishing line, Jeffry was breathing down her neck. "You are about to lose, Princess!" he snorted from behind.

Edelin gave everything she had until her legs turned to stone and crumpled beneath her, while her weighty load rolled on the ground.

Her wet eyes gazed up just as Jeffry crossed the line and gave her teammates a loathsome glance.

Only ten yards separated her from the end, but she failed her friends again. Edelin's spirit shattered into tiny pieces, and despair filled her heart.

Neither Tashunko nor Niro helped her to rise. They all knew Edelin must complete her part even if she lost. That was an important lesson the three of them had learned under the Ghosts. Never quit.

At last, she marched across the line with the barrel on her shoulders. Both Niro and Tashunko came to her side and encouraged her broken spirit.

"You gave your best, Edelin," Tashunko said with a smile.

"Not good enough!" She choked up with bitterness. Her lips were shaking, and tears trickled down her cheeks.

The thought of missing the Wizards' Game, after all the hell she'd gone through, ripped her young heart to pieces.

In her mind, she could see Zigler and Osmond mocking her. She could hear the story of her embarrassing defeat spreading throughout Low Earth.

"Edelin!" Niro seized her by the shoulders. "Focus only on the task ahead and nothing else. Nothing is over until it's over!" He stared at his companions with unshaken belief.

She wiped her tears and nodded with a forced smile. She had no confidence that they could turn the tables and win, so she rode on Niro's for now.

At last, they decided on the third contest—rapid shooting at a moving target. Each team member had fifteen seconds to pull arrows from a quiver and fire at a swinging wooden plate.

Jeffry and his friends were full of themselves as they strode to the line.

"Let's humiliate these losers one last time!" he sneered and mimicked Edelin's crying from before. "Didn't I tell you the Games are no place for a little girl?"

Her face showed no sign, yet it turned frosty like the Snowy Mountains of the North.

The first boy hit four targets. The second followed with three, and Jeffry finished with only two. They all seemed much pleased with their results and were confident that they had won the match.

"Nine hits for Jeffry's squad!" the master declared.

Niro, Tashunko, and Edelin exchanged swift smiles. At last, they realized how fortunate they were to be trained under the Ghost masters.

"Let's see you beating us now!" The boys and their friends laughed.

Niro went to the line and stood ready with his bow.

"Start!" the master called, and in fifteen seconds, he struck his target eight times.

A sudden silence followed, and everyone stood with their mouths open.

Tashunko ended with seven hits as the crowd murmured in awe. Then Edelin approached the line, readied her bow, and aimed.

"Stop!" the young master cried. Nine of her arrows had penetrated the wooden plate, and the cheering and whistles lasted for a long minute.

However, neither Edelin nor Niro nor Tashunko smiled. Jeffry's team was still leading two wins to one, and the boys were about to select the fourth one.

Now, all held their breath in anticipation.

"The next competition will be a full skirmish between the two teams!" Jeffry announced. "Each participant will choose from the following weapons: a six-foot pole which represents a spear, a shield and a wooden sword, or a pair of swords. The last one standing in the ring will win the contest for their team."

And so it was that Tashunko and Niro chose two swords each and Edelin a shield with a sword.

On the boys' team, the slender boy had a pole and a shield, and Jeffry and the other boy got a sword and a shield each.

"Begin!" thundered the young master, and loud cries followed.

Tashunko leaped toward Jeffry and roared like a raging lion, pounding his shield down with force. When the highborn finally dared to raise his head and attack, the Black Tongue blocked with his blades and kicked him to the ground. Stunned, Jeffry looked up to find the mighty Tashunko standing above him, his swords pointing at his neck.

In the meantime, Niro had been exchanging sword-strikes with the other boy, who defended himself quite well. Suddenly, Niro halted, and his foe stormed at him. He was waiting for just such a move. In a split second, Niro dodged to his left, slashed the unguarded side of his adversary, and swept the back of his ankle. He crashed on his back and yielded.

While Jeffry and his friend laid under Tashunko and Niro's feet, Edelin was fighting ferociously with the thin boy.

"Stay where you are!" she barked at her friends, who were ready to charge on her rival. "He is mine!"

She struck his shoulder, but he hit her on the thigh. Intense pain throbbed her leg, and she gave a cry and dropped to one knee.

Her opponent sprang forward with his pole, trying to knock her down, but she rolled to the side and escaped his blow. She sent a kick to the boy's knee, and he lost his balance. Next, the princess jumped to her feet and banged her shield on his face. At last, he sank on his backside, bleeding from the nose as she pressed her wooden blade against his throat.

"Victorious!" the master called.

Niro and Tashunko rushed to their teammate and lifted her high on their shoulders. The crowd whistled and yelled her name, and she noticed some of the boys smiling at her with respect.

Edelin's red dress was cut above the knees, and dust and sweat covered her skin. *No longer a princess,* she smiled to herself.

Again, this strange band of misfits had dominated Jeffry and his friends, and their bold faces turned nervous. Their leader joked no more, and wore an uptight smile on his face instead. The next and final contest would decide if he was about to lose face—and precious lands.

Niro eyed Jeffry like a tiger who studies his prey before the attack.

"Be ready for our next match!" he called out, but then he lowered his voice and whispered to Edelin and Tashunko. "Whatever you are about to hear, stay calm. Do not show the slightest hesitation or doubt, for our success depends only on that."

Before she and the Black Tongue had a chance to respond, he turned his back. A tense silence fell as Niro called out: "The closing event will be a test of high skill, courage, and trust. Teammates who have no faith in each other could never be a true team!" Niro's eyes skewered Jeffry. "The leader of each party will stand fifteen yards away from the shooting line with an apple on his head. A second member will try to hit the fruit. The one to succeed will win the fifth contest—and the bet!"

The crowd murmured with excitement and fear, and Jeffry stared at that cursed orphan with hateful eyes.

Edelin knew that Niro had challenged Jeffry's backbone and leadership in front of everybody. The pompous boy's face shifted colors from furious red to fearful white. He approached his friends, who gaped at him with mortified eyes.

"Edelin, take the bow!" Niro said as he walked away with an apple.

"Come back here, right now!" she snarled under her breath, and steam came out of her nostrils like a mad dragon. Niro turned and realized he had some explaining to do.

"Edelin, take the bow!" she mocked him, all enraged. "What are you doing? Do you have a death wish?" she grumbled heatedly. "Why don't you shoot and give me the apple instead, eh?"

"I would, Princess," he answered calmly. "But you are a better shot than me, especially on a steady target. During our practices, I watched you strike a coin at this distance!" His sapphire eyes twinkled at his friends, and the plan didn't seem so mad anymore.

"I picked this contest not only because I trust you to hit it, but because I am convinced Jeffry will not trust his teammate in this kind of a task."

It took long moments for the two to grasp Niro's words, but then smiles spread on their faces.

"To win a war without fighting, just by knowing your enemy's weakness," mumbled Tashunko with admiration.

"Edelin!" Niro said with a sharp note. "You did it before and you will do it again. Aim and fire if needed."

Minutes later, the crowd gathered near the shooting line. Behind it, the princess and the slender boy were ready with their bows, eight feet beside each other. Fifteen yards in front of them, Niro and Jeffry were standing still with apples on their heads.

"On my count from ten, prepare yourselves, but fire only on my mark!" the master instructed. "Ten…nine…eight…seven…"

"Edelin has done it many times before," Niro whispered to his rival indifferently.

"Shut your mouth!" Jeffry snarled, his eyes open wide. Cold sweat mantled his face.

"Six…five…"

"Your friend seemed a bit shaky. Are you sure he is up to the task?" Niro sounded as calm as though they were talking about the weather.

Jeffry puffed like a donkey as he gawked at his teammate. The bow seemed to sway in his hands, and his forehead had sheen under the light.

Edelin's arms were as steady as a statue, motionless. She aimed with confidence as Niro had told her.

"Four…three…two…one…"

"Stopppp!" Jeffry screamed and dropped on his knees.

His shaking hands covered his dripping face, and his legs turned into melted butter.

"Are you able to continue the match, or should I declare a winner?" The master asked, and all eyes gazed at him. The highborn shook his head, staring at the earth with humiliation. He decided to forfeit the bet.

At once, the crowd boomed and stormed the champions. They won the last battle and the entire war without a fight, all because of their leader's sharp mind.

Many of the boys, even their slender foe, came and congratulated each one of them on their victory.

"You are all incredible!"

"We are proud to have you in the Southern Team."

"Best of luck to you all."

"You are the toughest princess I have ever seen."

These were just a few of the praises they received that night.

***

The eating, drinking, and dancing resumed, and all were sitting together in one camp, including the boys from Capana Royalty Academy.

Later that night, the young master appeared with a parchment signed by Jeffry. The ranches south of Fluky Village would now belong to Tashunko's tribe.

Tashunko and Niro hugged each other happily. That piece of paper would change the lives of many in the Black Tongue clan.

The night grew dark but merry, and Edelin pulled Niro to the dancefloor. Her red dress was in tatters, but she cared not, spinning on her bare feet like a little girl. Suddenly, she dived into his sapphire sparkling eyes and kissed him softly on his lips.

"Thank you for tonight. You were brilliant like the northern star!" She smiled and dashed back to the girls. The maidens' giggles and blushes hastened Niro out of the circle.

It caught him by surprise and stirred his head and his heart. *This might complicate things,* he thought, yet he embraced the warm sensation that went through his body when he thought about their kiss.

His mind roamed as he wandered the yard, but suddenly he froze. A shadow stood under an oak tree to his right. It was Jeffry.

He had been gazing at him in the dark, all by himself. A moment later, he marched to Niro.

Niro's hands clenched into mighty fists, and all of his muscles became tense.

The highborn halted just in front of him and scanned his rival's face. Yet Niro sensed no animosity. Only respect…

"Good luck in the Wizards' Game," he nodded with a half-smile and went away.

Jeffry left Niro with a frozen tongue, for it came on him like a storm on a bright day. Puzzled and stunned, he strolled through the trees, searching for Tashunko.

At last, he found him under a tree's branches, but he was not alone. His brother was kissing a girl in a white dress, and when he sneaked closer, he saw it was none other than Olivia.

"What a night..." he chuckled in disbelief and headed back to the party.

About midnight, Edelin, Niro, Tashunko, and Olivia strode back to the house, singing and laughing. That was an unforgettable night, indeed.

At dawn, the team waited in the lower field, as usual, ready for their short warm-up with Ganix. He darted suspicious glances behind him and watched the three burst into laughter as they relived their adventurous contest from the night before.

When they climbed up the mountain, Ronald was waiting for them. His face was chilled.

They exchanged anxious glimpses, praying he hadn't discovered the stolen wine barrels from last night.

"Edelin," he spoke with a worried voice, "your Royal Falcon has just arrived with an urgent message."

He handed her a letter, and she unfolded it with nervous fingers.

My beloved daughter,

I wish I could say it more softly, but nothing comes to my head.

Your father is dying and perhaps has only a few weeks to live. He whispered your name many times and asked to see you before he passes to the afterlife.

Please be safe but swift.

Love, Mother

The princess stared at the message in disbelief, reading it again, yet the bad news remained.

"I don't understand..." she whimpered with trembling lips. "He seemed to be getting better..."

Tears fell on the letter, and her body turned weak and brittle under the weighty words. A moment later, she collapsed on the ground.

Ronald carried her swiftly to the house with the boys and Ganix behind him.

"What happened?" Tashunko asked his brother, who read the letter with sad eyes.

"It's her father… King Wilfred is dying," Niro sighed. The Black Tongue and the master trainer looked at each other without a word.

When Edelin opened her eyes, she seemed embarrassed.

"I am sorry, Ronald…" she muttered. He just smiled warmly and gave her some water. After all of these months of training and adventures, she had become like a daughter to him.

"No worries, my dear." He patted her hair. "I will take you to the harbor today. There is a ship that sails directly to the North."

"We will join her!" Niro said at once. "Regardless, we are supposed to sail for the Wizards' Game soon, which will be held in the Northern arena."

The winemaker was considering the proposition, and Tashunko nodded with agreement.

"We've already completed our main training," Niro pressed at his master, "and it will help her to be with us during the long voyage."

Ronald glanced at Edelin's sad face and knew the boy was right. Her teammates could ease her sadness and pain.

"So be it," he said swiftly. "Prepare yourselves; we are leaving in an hour!"

CHAPTER 11

UNEXPECTED ALLIES

Half-Lip stood in the dark room with a shaking pillow in his hands. His forehead dripped sweat as he was staring at the puzzled Bloody Shirt who gaped back at him.

"What are you doing here, boy?" The red-haired man snarled with a threatening voice.

"I just ca…came to see if you are okay," Half-Lip's tongue stuttered. "I brought you a pillow."

The guard seized it and shoved it behind his back, still gazing at the boy.

"I injured my shoulder in practice, so the healer kept me here," Half-Lip explained with an apologetic voice.

The Bloody Shirt squinted. "Did you fight in the arena yet?"

"No, sir…" the boy's voice trembled.

"Your accent… Where are you from, lad?"

"I am from the South. One night, we were all kidnaped from our shelter, the Four Miracles Castle."

"I heard stories about that place…" The man gave an unexpected smile. "Perhaps you know two friends of mine, Alec and Lia."

Half-Lip's jaw dropped to the floor, and his eyes lit the dark room like two moons.

"How is it possible?" He mumbled, stunned. "Are they here?"

"Slowly, my boy!" The Bloody Shirt's eyes sparkled now. "If you are familiar with those two, then you must be a friend." Then, the man scanned the room, making sure the other beds were empty.

"My name is Rusty, and I am no Bloody Shirt," he said. Half-Lip stared at the man's uniform in confusion. "These are not my clothes. Let's say that I borrowed them for the meantime."

"Sir…" the boy murmured with glinting eyes. "You were talking in your sleep and called a name, Captain Quint! I am a good friend of his son, Niro! Do you know him? Is his father alive?" Half-Lip asked without taking a breath.

"Yes, he is, and more than ever." Rusty smiled, and the boy leapt for joy. He wanted to shout, for the news made his heart sing. But then he recalled they were still captives on this dreadful island.

For the next hours, Rusty told him everything that had happened out on the ocean: about the *Skulls Cleaver*, how he saved Alec, and the night he got trapped on the Navy ship.

"When I couldn't slip away, I hid and dressed as one of the Bloody Shirts," Rusty explained. "Fortunately, new men are arriving here all the time, so no one asked me tough questions. Soon enough, I found myself in Lord Marlo Eckhart's fortress. Last night, I became sick and came here for the healer to get treatment." Suddenly, Rusty's face seemed worried.

"What is it, sir?"

"I must be on my feet again, or many of the slaves below will be hungry tonight," Rusty answered with frustration.

"So you are the Red Angel!" Half-Lip called with a smile. "The Bloody Shirt who brings food for the slaves. I've heard all about you!"

The man gave him a puzzled gaze.

"That is what they call you down there!" He laughed. "You gave them hope and light in this dark hell."

The boy noted the sparkle in Rusty's blue eyes as though he realized his own deeds for the first time.

The night went on, and the two exchanged more tales. "What is this island for?" Half-Lip finally asked. "Why are the Bloody Shirts bringing so many slaves here?"

Rusty measured him for a while. "I trusted Alec and Lia, and so I will do with you. From what I learned around me, and from the bits of information I gathered for the last weeks, this hidden land in the Treacherous Sea is used to conceal a secret Army and Navy. According to the Bloody Shirts, there are many training camps around. In addition, the harbor hides dozens of warships.

"The part we are in is the entertainment and mining region of the island. Here, slaves mine in the mountains for silver and gold, and the chosen warriors like yourself fight in battles of life and death for the amusement of thousands in the arena." Rusty's voice became bitter, and his eyes spat fire.

"Thousands?" Half-Lip mumbled in disbelief.

Rusty nodded with a disgusted face.

"You see, more than a century ago, before the Guardians came to protect Low Earth, the Blood Games were the most popular spectacle in the lands. But after the wizards trounced our enemies and won the Great War, everything changed. Together with the young Wolf King, Bert Lukos, they agreed that no blood would be spilled for the sake of entertainment. Since that year, they banned all sorts of barbarous contests.

"The Guardians also outlawed other prevailing customs and practices, such as any kind of slavery and brutality against animals. These new laws were supposed to advance Low Earth into a golden age of arts, culture, and poetry—instead of barbarism, suffering, and violence. Nevertheless, not all embraced the new reforms.

"Many of the affluent lords and wealthy landowners depended on slaves and needed them to increase their wealth. Some had manipulated the Blood Games to promote their popularity while others used the sport to distract the commoners and poor from the real difficulties in their lives. Now, these nobles and Prince Zigler's allies have found a place to fulfill their sickening and brutal desires.

"In the secret island of death, they became the only masters. This is a lawless land, where enough gold buys slaves, warriors, and, above all, blood sport. Once again, they live as their ancestors did, before the days of the wizards."

A long silence followed Rusty's words, and Half-Lip strode to and fro in the dark.

"But how is it that no one knows about the island?"

"The lords are all highly secretive and associate only among themselves. Dozens of Navy ships, commanded by the Bloody Shirts, pick them up from a secured harbor on the northern shore. Once they cross the Frosty Reef, they are untouchable. No captain in his right mind would risk sailing into the Treacherous Sea, not even the legendary Robin Quint. I am certain he couldn't believe his own eyes when he watched the ships crossing the Frosty Reef. This island is hidden and guarded better than anyone can imagine."

Rusty sank on the pillows and sighed. "How did it come to this?" He shook his head and muttered under his breath, but Half-Lip grasped the words.

"Who is behind all of this?" the boy asked.

"Zigler is the primary suspect. He is the prince of the Northern Kingdom and a dangerous, cunning man. No blood flows in his body, just deadly venom. And the Bloody Shirts are his fanatic followers. Nonetheless, he is not the only one involved. Others aid him in this plot."

"I thought King Wilfred was an honorable man. How did he allow this to happen?"

"The Wolf King is a trustworthy man, and I would bet my life that he doesn't know anything about his son's deeds. For the last nine years, we heard he had been sick, handing all power to his elder son. Soon enough, Zigler took control of the government and appointed his loyal men throughout the Army and Navy." Just then, Rusty yawned and handed the pillow back to Half-Lip. "All right, I've had enough for one night, my lad! You should get some rest. The rumors say that thousands of zealous spectators are expected to arrive here on the island in the next few days. And that means only one thing—prepare yourself for a battle."

A ruthless fear seized Half-Lip's mind as he dragged himself back to his bed. For an hour, he lay on the bed with his eyes open while Rusty's last words echoed in his head: *Prepare yourself for a battle.*

***

The sound of keys clanging behind the door woke Half-Lip up. A moment after, the door opened and the healer dashed inside, carrying a tray.

"Some food for you both." He passed a bowl of porridge for each.

They thanked him as he stared at Rusty and touched his forehead. "Ahh…the fever is almost broken!" He sounded content. Then he gave Half-Lip a swift glance. "And you, boy, how is your shoulder?"

"Much better. Not aching at all!"

"Oh good, very good!" The old man smiled. "Gorgos will be pleased. He urged me to treat you until you are ready. A grand show is planned in the arena, and they need the best warriors from each camp."

The boy turned as white as the bedding he sat upon. The liveliness of the morning departed his body, and the fears of last night wrapped him like a thick blanket, blocking out the light and the hope.

Suddenly, the healer dashed to the door and departed, saying, "I will be back shortly…"

"Half-Lip!" Rusty snapped. He seemed quite different this morning, his face intense and determined. "Cast out all fears, or you die swiftly in the ring. If they pick you to fight, show confidence." His dark blue eyes skewered the lad. "You must survive until I find a way to escape this hell.

The healer returned a moment later. "You can go back to your training!" he said. Half-Lip thanked him and departed the room.

On his way to the practice court, he passed the dining area. Cler was washing dishes with a grim face, but as she noticed him, a soft smile curled on her mouth and kindled his heart. *I have another reason to survive now,* he thought to himself.

All morning, Half-Lip practiced with swords. He defeated a few of his opponents with ease, and a new conviction boosted his spirit.

His brother Dabi darted troubled glances at him while Gorgos watched nearby, correcting their techniques.

At lunch, the siblings were standing in line for food.

"It feels good to train again," Half-Lip smiled. "I have much to tell you!"

Rather than a smile, his mute brother gave him an elbow and gestured nervously at two faces that watched the morning practice. The men were standing beside Gorgos, and they were all murmuring.

"They were picking warriors to fight," Half-Lip mumbled, and the twinkle vanished from his eyes. "I am such a fool!" He muttered under his breath. Throughout the training, Dabi had motioned for him to slow down, but he didn't grasp it. Instead, he was fighting with purpose and passion, drawing too much attention to himself.

"Are you certain?" Half-Lip asked. His brother nodded and pointed a finger to his ears. He had heard them talking.

Half-Lip gave a miserable sigh and walked by Gorgos and two men, sensing their gazes on his back.

At lunch, Half-Lip told Dabi all about Rusty and last night's events, including the kiss with Cler. Dabi's eyes glinted, probing for more details. For half an hour, it felt like they were back in the Four Miracles Castle and had no burden on their shoulders.

When they returned to the practice court, Gorgos summoned all of them.

"Tomorrow, some of you will fight your first battle in the arena!" he called, and the warriors all exchanged nervous glances, praying to their gods not to hear their names.

"Vas! Half-Lip! Milan! Step forward!" the master trainer commanded proudly. "You have been chosen!"

The three paced ahead, the scent of death glued to every breath they took. Half-Lip stared at his brother, whose heart seemed to be ripped to pieces.

"Gorgos! Come here!" Lord Eckhart suddenly appeared, and the baldheaded trainer bolted to him. For long moments, they spoke to each other, throwing looks at the warriors.

At last, he came back, and Half-Lip prayed for a miracle. Perhaps they had changed their mind and didn't need him.

"Tight-Lip!" Gorgos called, for this was the name he had given the mute brother. "Come forward. You shall be our fourth warrior in the arena."

As Half-Lip's heart sank to the sand, Dabi stood beside him and smiled. He seemed quite relieved to join his brother, no matter the consequences. Next, Gorgos directed the others to drill while he signaled the four to follow him.

They rushed through the fortress's half-open corridors until they reached the armory. A sweaty, porky man measured each of them and gave them light armor. Then he brought them steel swords and wooden shields.

Gorgos led them out to a small training ground, where a few of the Bloody Shirts were practicing. As they noticed him, they all cleared the space and cheered eagerly for the four chosen warriors.

For the next several hours, Gorgos faced each one, highlighting their weaknesses and strengths. The sounds of clashing steel made them each shiver, for they had been accustomed to the wooden swords—but in no time, the thrill took over and they turned fearless.

"Tomorrow, you will fight against four of Lord Priskos's warriors," Gorgos said quietly. "He is one of the wealthiest lords and known for paying many coins to buy the best candidates. Some of his men are murderers and thieves, and others are ex-soldiers who seek fame and riches. All have tasted blood before."

Half-Lip felt the sweat pouring under his helmet. The only battle experience he'd known was fighting his own father, and that didn't end well for his lips.

"It is almost certain that they are better fighters than you," Gorgos added indifferently. "However, they are not disciplined and fight only for glory, not caring for their companions. If you fight as a team, you give yourselves a chance. If not, you will all fall."

With these dark words, they resumed their training, but now they practiced as a group. Gorgos ordered a few Bloody Shirts to attack them from different directions while the warriors shielded each other and fought together.

"You slimy dogs!" a sudden loud curse sounded near the obstacle course. Three Bloody Shirts were dragging two noisy pirates who had recently been taken prisoner. One of the Bloody Shirts lashed them hard, and one of the captives spat in his face.

By now, everyone was following the little commotion. The humiliated guard growled like a madman and drew his dagger. He was about to cut the prisoner's throat when another Bloody Shirt raced from the side and jumped on the prisoners, knocking them to the ground. He began beating both with his mighty fists to the amusement of the cheering guards.

Half-Lip and Dabi watched as the whole scene unfolded.

***

Neal and Pozzo cowered as the Bloody Shirt wailed upon them with his fists. But even though his blows seemed violent and devastating, somehow, they never landed with much force.

Stunned, Neal and Pozzo were staring with wide-open eyes at Rusty.

"I will teach you a lesson you won't forget!" he barked furiously and winked at the two pirates.

"When you finish with these fools, throw them into the shittiest cell you can find," the guard snorted and put his knife back in its sheath.

Rusty pulled the two prisoners through the courtyard. "Faster, you pigs, or I'll peel your filthy skin!" he thundered as the Bloody Shirts laughed.

"Rusty!" Neal whispered in disbelief as he played along, stumbling and pretending to be badly hurt. "It's a miracle to see you alive!"

They marched in the dim corridor as he led them into their new cell.

"It's good to see you both, shipmates!" Rusty's eyes sparkled, and he seemed to be surprised by how happy he was to see them again. He handed them a piece of bread and strips of dried salty beef from his pocket. "Here, take this for now."

"Bless your heart!" Neal smiled, and the two grabbed the food like starving wolves.

"These bastards starved us on the ship!" Pozzo snapped.

The sounds of heavy steps echoed as they began to ask more questions.

"I will come later once darkness falls!" Rusty said, and he hurried back the way he'd come.

***

At night, the Red Angel visited the underground slave pens, handing them food, and encouraging smiles. From there, he sneaked up to the warriors' dungeon and found Neal and Pozzo, standing like sentinels.

Their eyes glinted in the dark as he approached the bars to their cell. The guards didn't enter the building at night, so he could be there with no one to spot him. He brought them some leftovers from dinner.

Without delay, Rusty told them all that had happened to him, and his discoveries about the island, the slaves, and more.

"How is it that they captured only the two of you?" He asked suspiciously. "Where is the *Skulls Cleaver* and the rest of the crew? Where is Quint?"

Pozzo's eyes rattled like a mouse, looking at the Eel to lie and save their necks—for now.

"After the cursed night you were trapped on the Navy ship," Neal explained, "the *Skulls Cleaver* remained at a distance for a few weeks, waiting for your return. When you didn't come back, the captain decided to make sail toward the Bone Isles.

"Soon enough, we approached a group of islands. Robin sent us two in a skiff to reconnoiter, for we were familiar with the area. But as we got closer, a Navy ship surprised us from the south. We had no choice but to surrender."

Pozzo swallowed a chunk of bread and scanned Rusty's face.

"Do not test the Bloody Shirts' tolerance again," Rusty said, believing the story that Neal had told him. "During my short time here, I have witnessed too many throats slit. I need you alive so we can escape this hell."

The Eel nodded and thanked him for saving their lives. On his way back, Rusty passed Half-Lip's cell for a final chat before the arena battle tomorrow, but to his surprise, it was empty.

The time was about three hours before midnight, and his mind started guessing where the two brothers could be.

CHAPTER 12

KISSES AND BLOOD

By the time the chosen warriors finished their training with Gorgos, it was evening. The master trainer ushered them to the top floor, where the highborn family and honorable guests resided.

Suddenly, they halted in the upstairs hallway as Lord Eckhart approached them. He was tall and lean. His crow-black eyes and hair contrasted with his pale, white skin. It seemed as though the sun had never laid its rays upon his face.

He studied the four faces for a brief moment and dug hard for a smile deep beneath his frozen expression. A twist of his lips was the best he managed.

"Tomorrow, you will fight for your life in the arena, but tonight you will be spoiled like kings. Prove to me that you are worthy, and I will show you fame and richness beyond imagination!" With that, he turned back to his chamber.

They stood in utter silence. Half-Lip couldn't believe that this unattractive man had such charisma. Like the companions beside him, goosebumps covered his skin, and he almost got excited.

"Lord Eckhart always delivers what he promises," Gorgos said with respect. "Especially this time, when he battles his most hated rival, Lord Priskos."

Rather than returning to the warriors' cells, he led each one to a private guest room.

He smiled at Half-Lip.

"You will sleep here tonight," he said and left.

Half-Lip scanned his grand room with stunned eyes. A luxurious bed stood opposite a burning fireplace, and a table loaded with kingly dishes was set beside the balcony. A cool evening breeze blew through the doors and rustled the white curtains. The smell of spicy roasted chicken and grilled meat filled his nose, and his mouth salivated like a famished dog.

Near the window, steam rose from a round washtub. Half-Lip dipped his fingers in the pleasant water, and his mind turned quiet. An aroma of spring blossoms permeated the room, and the lad inhaled with a smile.

As he soaked himself in the friendly water, his sore legs and stiff shoulders sighed in relief. If not for his rumbling stomach, he would have rested in the tub till dawn.

Finally, he put on a clean robe and dragged himself to the laden table, debating where to start.

A chunk of roasted chicken met his tongue when a faint knock sounded at the door. Next, a young woman dressed in a silky white dress entered the dim room carrying a tray with fruits and wine. As she stepped closer to the light, the food fell from his wide-open mouth.

"Cler?" He said softly, and the maiden almost dropped the platter. "What are you doing here?"

"Oh, Half-Lip, I am so glad it's you!" she sobbed and slumped on the floor.

The boy jumped off his chair and knelt beside her.

"Everything is all right now…" He hugged her warmly.

For long minutes, Cler sniffled on his chest until she finally calmed down.

"Why are you here?" She asked with a tremulous voice.

"I've been chosen to fight in the arena tomorrow, together with Dabi and two other Warriors." Half-Lip shrugged. "Lord Eckhart decided to spoil us in his guest rooms. I guess it is his way to motivate us, as though fighting for our life is not enough."

"That's terrible!" Cler covered her mouth, horrified. "And here I am sobbing selfishly when you are the ones to face death tomorrow." Guilt clasped her voice. "They commanded three other slave girls and me to serve you wine and food and fulfill all of your desires…"

Tears trickled down her face, and she was trembling like a leaf on a windy day. Half-Lip realized what she meant, and his eyes blazed with anger and hate.

"These bastards!" he growled and bolted out to the balcony. He leaped to the adjacent balconies and burst into Vas's and Milan's rooms like a lightning storm, carrying his message to them.

"Don't you dare force yourself on these girls, or you will become my enemy tomorrow!" he threatened and left them with stunned faces.

When he returned, Cler was gazing at him.

"Thank you, Half-Lip." Her eyes glinted like bright stars, for she had heard what he said to the others.

"Let's enjoy the food before it turns cold," he smiled and sat down.

She stopped him with a foxy smile, taking food with her fingers and feeding him.

"They asked me to pamper you like a king, so let me do my work." She had a mysterious gaze in her eyes, while Half-Lip obeyed like a child.

The young evening grew into an adult night, and what started with crying and sadness continued with laughter. They sat beside the crackling fire and reminded each other about adventures and stories from the shelter. Soon enough, the boy was dozing, and Cler led him to bed.

"Go to sleep now. Tomorrow you need to be at your best," she whispered and stroked his hair.

A few racing heartbeats later, Half-Lip's tired eyes opened like an owl as she slid under the blankets.

She wiggled herself closer, and the touch of her naked body against his back made his heart explode. The rose scent on her skin traveled through his nostrils and drove him mad. Her warm breath on his neck sounded like an ancient spell.

Half-Lip turned and kissed her soft lips. They were shivering with excitement, for it was their first experience.

"Are you sure about this?" he asked directly. He wanted to clear his conscious of any doubt.

"Am I sure?" Cler whispered. "I was truly fortunate to meet you here. If it was someone else, I would have carried the painful memory every day to the end of my life. They tried to take everything from me. But the blessed gods brought us together, in this room, filling my heart with love and hope. Instead of a lasting scar, I will cherish these moments in your arms forever, no matter what tomorrow brings." Cler's smile kindled her face, and she kissed him again.

"At least I wouldn't die a virgin," the boy mumbled out loud, and they burst in laughter.

That night turned precious for them both. Sharing young love in the darkest place of all gave them some promise.

***

The morning came, and all the warriors assembled on the training ground. Blue sky stretched over their heads, and Half-Lip gazed at it sadly. None of them might enjoy this beauty again—not him, not his brother, not his friends. The wind caressed his cheeks, and the rising sun gave some warmth.

It's strange, he thought. *I sense ordinary things with more intensity and appreciation when I am about to lose them all.*

Gorgos's voice brought him back.

"The battle will start at midday! All of you will accompany and encourage your brothers who fight today. In addition, Lord Eckhart has decided that our two new warriors will join the chosen four."

Gorgos pointed at Pozzo and Neal, who had been in the middle of yawning.

"Do you mean us…fighting in the arena?" Neal called, suddenly confused. "We just arrived yesterday. We were starved half to death on the voyage here. We're not yet ready to fight!"

Gorgos glared at him with burning eyes and charged like a raging bull. "Another word, and I will send you there with no weapons at all!" he barked and sprayed like a skunk.

The Eel measured him with cold eyes and knew they had no choice.

"As you say, master trainer…" Neal answered respectfully, and Gorgos returned to his place, pleased.

The Blood Games began at noon, and thousands of people were cheering as every warrior entered the arena. Lord Eckhart's six warriors were waiting restlessly in the lower level, each one lost in his own dreadful thoughts.

The crowd noise from above made their anxious hearts bang like drums. Their poor guts twisted like frightened snakes, and they vomited one after the other. Time crawled, and the anxiety and stress became unbearable.

Even the Eel, who had fought in many battles before, seemed edgy. Suddenly, Half-Lip recalled what Rusty had told him and Dabi that morning.

"Stay close to Neal at all times," the red-haired pirate had said. "He was trained as a Sea Ghost before he turned into a pirate. And as far as I remember, he mastered the sword as well as his sharp tongue."

It was against Gorgos's advice, but Half-Lip had learned to trust Rusty's intuition.

Meantime, in the arena, the warriors of the other lords had been fighting for their lives, some in one-to-one combat, others in pairs and groups. A few unlucky ones battled wild beasts with just a knife or a spear. The blows of many horns shook the seats, and the sounds of running boots reached their cell.

A group of Bloody Shirts opened the door and accompanied them up to the entrance to the arena. One of them was Rusty, who gave the two boys and his former shipmates a last encouraging smile before they dashed onto the battleground.

Deafening cheering and clapping surrounded the six warriors who walked out onto the bloody sand with goosebumps of fear and adrenaline. They stared in disbelief at the raging multitude around them while Lord Priskos's champions marched with confidence and waved to the crowd with cheerful cries.

Half-Lip watched his team stepping with hesitant feet through bloody puddles. The golden sand couldn't absorb the hours of bloodbath and horror. Of their six, three were younger than eighteen, and Half-Lip's heart told him they were in deep trouble.

A balcony decorated with banners stood high in the middle of the seats. He caught a glimpse of the nobles, sitting on comfortable chairs. Slaves were serving them wine and delicacies, as they were ready to watch men slaughtering each other.

Half-Lip and Dabi followed Neal and Pozzo until they reached the center of the arena. There, Eckhart's six warriors stood in line and stared at Lord Priskos's men. They seemed powerful and cruel under their armor, and a few of them started laughing.

"Take a look; they sent us a few piglets to slaughter!" One of them chuckled viciously and licked his sharp ax. A stream of blood dripped from his tongue, down to his neck. The man looked like a Bloodsucker, and Half-Lip grabbed Vas's arm, which trembled in fear.

"Stay strong! We must stick together!" he whispered.

A horn suddenly blew, and the announcer shrieked, "Begin!"

The crowd cheered, and Priskos's men charged at them like wild bulls. The two brothers stood their ground and defended themselves with shields and swords. To their left, Neal and Pozzo pounded their opponents.

Only half a minute into the battle, the formation of Eckhart's warriors collapsed. Half-Lip held his ground against the mighty slashes of his enemy, but his left arm that raised the shield in front shivered with pain anytime his rival struck.

On his right, he caught a glimpse of Vas and Milan falling to the ground. A moment later, a sword and a spear pierced through their chests, and their deafening screams filled the battleground. Blood gushed from their wounds and seeped into the puddles already on the ground.

Startled by death closing in on them, Half-Lip jumped on his opponent and whacked his shield into the man's helmet. The stunned man retreated, hardly able to keep his balance, and so Half-Lip attacked Dabi's foe from the side and slashed his leg. His brother's combatant howled and limped away. Half-Lip pulled Dabi forward until they were back-to-back with Neal and Pozzo.

Vas and Milan lay dead on the sand as the six snarling warriors circled them.

"That's it; stay together!" the Eel spoke. He was the only one without a shield, but he had two swords.

Suddenly, two men sprang at him, yet he was faster. In a swift motion, he slashed the first man's arm and dodged a swing from an ax. Then, with his other hand, he sliced the unprotected thigh of the other. Both wailed and sank to the ground, and he thrust his blades in their chests.

Pozzo, Half-Lip, and Dabi were still standing back-to-back, protecting each other as Neal resumed his attack. He seized the ax and hurled it at the foe who stormed at him from his left. A harsh snap sounded, and that warrior fell on his back, twitching.

The crowd grew louder, for the show exceeded their expectations. Now, the warrior that Half-Lip had wounded leaped from the side to stab Neal's back. Fortunately for the captain, Pozzo's blade met him first.

Neal glanced backward to find the warrior crashing on his face. His sword only scratched the Eel.

Emboldened, the brothers attacked the remaining two warriors until they overpowered them—Half-Lip delivering a sharp thrust to the chest and Dabi landing a blow to the head.

The thousands of onlookers in the arena were standing in astonishment, and except for little murmurings, no one spoke or cheered. Nevertheless, at the lavish balcony, Lord Eckhart was clapping, screaming, and whistling like a fanatic.

"The winner is the House of Eckhart!" the announcer called, and the stunned spectators cheered non-stopped for minutes. Though most of them had lost many coins on their bet, they admired the excellent show.

"Bow to the crowd!" Neal said. "We have to win them over before we can get out of this hell."

The four warriors bobbed their heads in all directions, and the crowd applauded even more.

As the guards rushed into the battleground, Half-Lip gazed at Neal. "Captain Eel, we are forever in your debt."

That was the last skirmish of the day, and everyone was talking about it as they poured out of the arena. Rusty beamed as he accompanied them back to the fortress.

The two pirates and both brothers passed through the gate when loud cheering sounded from the Bloody Shirts on the walls.

"It cannot be..." Gorgos mumbled when Lord Eckhart trotted on his horse with a real smile on his face. He had a custom not to go to the arena when his trainees fought.

"Gorgos!" Marlo Eckhart called cheerfully. "You should see Priskos's face, whining like a baby. Summon everyone now!" he ordered.

The master trainer gathered everyone in the training court.

Lord Eckhart scanned the faces and bellowed from his mount. "Today was a glorious day in the arena for our brotherhood!" His eyes landed on Neal, Pozzo, and the boys. "These four lions fought with courage and skill, and they will be rewarded handsomely. Tonight, we shall feast to celebrate this glorious victory!"

Everyone in the courtyard banged their swords.

***

In a matter of minutes, the rumors about the tremendous triumph spread throughout the fortress, and the champions were instantly famous. People and guards stared at them with awe as they told their own versions of the battle.

At the feast, they all were devouring the abundant food and fine wine while Lord Eckhart and Gorgos were standing ten feet from the winners' table, watching Neal.

"You should have seen him fighting!" Marlo chuckled. "This man has some skill with blades. He killed three of Priskos's warriors as though they were children."

"How did the boys fight?" the master trainer asked, changing the subject.

"Like wolves!" Eckhart roared. "They defended hard and struck down much more experienced fighters."

A broad grin curled on Gorgos's face, for he was fond of the two brothers.

"At last, luck is on our side…" the lord sighed and gazed at the glinting stars.

Of all the nobles, he was considered one of the inferiors. Most of his peers disrespected him on many occasions, particularly the arrogant Priskos.

"The bet was one-to-fifteen against us," Eckhart broke the silence. "Last night was the first night ever that I dreamed about a battle, and in my dream, we won the skirmish. I decided to listen to my heart and wager more than 200 gold coins on our team."

Gorgos's stiff jaw plunged to the floor, and so did his cup of wine. "Did I hear you right, my lord?

"You heard me damn well, Gorgos!" The pale man chortled, and the red drink splashed on his shirt. "Tonight, I became one of the richest men on this island. Let's see who the laughingstock is, now, eh?" He laughed again, and both men drank from their cups.

Next, they walked to the table where Neal, Pozzo, and the two boys had been sitting. The four were eating and drinking merrily when Eckhart and Gorgos approached. The warriors rose to their feet and bowed slightly.

"Sit down..." The lord spoke with a friendly tone and smiled at his golden hens. He beamed at the Eel, not even knowing his name. "Where did you learn to fight?"

"Neal, at your service, sir," he said swiftly. "My father taught me to battle with a sword since I was a boy, and the rest I learned from the pirates."

Gorgos and Eckhart exchanged suspicious glances. Eckhart smelled a lie, but he pushed it no further.

"Then I will toast to both your father and the Bastards!" he thundered. "Their efforts have made this day a celebration for us all." The warriors and the Bloody Shirts around cheered and drank their wine.

***

During the feast, Rusty hurried through the slaves' corridor. He carried full bags of delicious food from the celebration, handing out bread and chickens and other meat. At once, the bony cheeks in the cells murmured with excitement.

"The Red Angel is here!"

"Bless your kind heart, sir!"

"Thank you! You give us hope."

That night, the slaves had their own banquet, feeding their empty stomachs with rich food as the Red Angel's chest filled with joy.

"A good day," Rusty mumbled as his eyes twinkled in the dark.

CHAPTER 13

MAGIC IN THE CASTLE

Infinite bright stars glinted in the black sky as Elmagos led the wizards through forests and meadows and across streams and rivers. At last, the giant white statues of Norvita appeared under the moonlight.

The cool evening breeze sent chills down their spines. They gazed in awe at the Cloak Castle, recalling the last visit inside. Soon enough, the three hooded men entered the city. The hour was late, and the clatter of hooves resonated through Norvita's empty streets. They tied their horses near Pafos's and Kayra's monument. Elmagos surveyed the soundless street for a while. When he found no shadows out and about, he hastened with his brothers into the crypt.

Inside, they opened the secret door and vanished into the underground passage. In utter silence, they ascended the steep steps all the way up to the chamber between the Wizard's Feet.

Elmagos watched his brothers' eyes brim with astonishment and sadness as they strode through the dark building. Mold and mustiness covered the walls, and dust puffed with any step they took until they soared on the wooden eagle to the top of the Leg. He heard only their gasps as they crossed the classrooms and grand library in the Torso. At last, the somber company climbed the Neck's hidden stairs up to the Head.

Suddenly, Laos the Orange stopped dead in the hall. He whispered, and a tiny whirl of dust swept the floor around them.

"We should bring this graveyard back to what it used to be!" he uttered with glowing eyes.

As though his words cracked a dam that held back a gushing river, the gloom turned into excitement.

"Yes! We will restore it room by room!" Petri the Blue declared with a smile.

"I will find a book with all the spells we need," said Laos, "for I have forgotten most of them."

"Blazomos!" Petri cried, and red sparks pierced the darkness and kindled the two fireplaces in the room.

Elmagos stood silent. The two stared at him, studying his face.

"I think it's a brilliant idea. We shall start in the morning, then."

All hearts pumped lively blood through their bodies as they climbed the staircase.

At that moment, a shadow sped through the upstairs hallway and stopped in front of them.

"Elmagos!" Kordos's voice sang with excitement. "Welcome back!"

Laos and Petri froze and gave the boy frosty glances. They had not forgotten how he turned into a curse back in Magisol.

Elmagos, however, embraced him warmly.

"Did you find anything unusual?" the green cloak whispered with a smile.

"Not one, but many!" answered the lad. He bowed to the two other wizards as they passed by him.

"Tomorrow morning, we shall restore the Cloak Castle to its glorious age." Elmagos squinted at Kordos. "I sense that in my absence, you learned some new things. Perhaps you might be useful, after all. All right, my lad, I go to sleep now. An exciting day awaits us!" He winked and disappeared behind the door.

"Good night, my wizard…"

***

The sun came through the balcony and flooded Seros's room with morning light. Kordos woke up and sat on his bed. Sounds of dragging furniture and men's voices came from the hallway.

He stepped out of his room and rubbed his mesmerized eyes in disbelief. *I must be dreaming,* he thought.

Around him, mops were cleaning the floors, brushes scrubbing the sticky green moss from walls and ceilings, and brooms and buckets were hovering and washing the surfaces vigorously.

With his mouth open wide, Kordos walked along the bedrooms, gaping at Petri chanting spells while jars and books floated near him.

In the library, he noted Laos holding a book, commanding saws and hammers to fix broken tables and chairs, windows, and doors. The boy continued to roam speechlessly, witnessing the incredible magic everywhere.

Long hours passed before Kordos reached the garden at the top of the statue. The ground had seen as much action as the chambers underneath.

Shovels and pitchforks were digging, rakes were raking, and shears and axes were cutting. Soon enough, the strangling weeds of the past turned into a fine breathing space, ready for new plants.

In the midst of all this, Kordos's eyes caught wisps of smoke floating from the west side and headed toward them. He found the three cloaks, sitting and laughing on the restored patio near the purple tree. They were studying some books on charms.

"At last, you decided to join the workforce!" Elmagos announced.

"I am working as hard as you three!" the boy replied sarcastically, and they all laughed.

The men got back to their smoking and conversation, and Kordos strolled aimlessly. A minute after, he reached the western boundary of the garden, the closest spot to the Crown Castle.

For a while, he craned over the railing at Norvita's streets far below. His curious eyes swept the buildings, guessing what each was for.

Suddenly, he heard voices. He peeked behind him but found nothing. A few heartbeats later, the sounds came again.

To his utter surprise, they came from the garden at the Crown Castle.

Swiftly, Kordos lay on the ground. The voices sounded much clearer now, and a strange thought went through his mind. When he peeped through the balustrades, his heart stopped at once.

Standing behind the Crown Garden's railings, beneath the many cherry trees, were none other than Niro, Tashunko, and Evert. A beautiful maiden stood beside the prince. Her face was similar to the queen's.

Kordos seemed confused. He wanted to talk with his friends, but he knew he had to be secretive about his presence in the Cloak Castle. Nevertheless, his legs didn't obey as he rose to his feet, waving at the astonished faces on the other side.

"It's good to see you again, strangers!" He spoke just enough for the words to meet them. The four figures gaped at him as though they had just seen a ghost.

"Kordos?" Evert's eyes turned twice as large. "How did you get there, for heaven's sake?

"Kordos!" Niro and Tashunko boomed together once they finally discovered their tongues. The young woman with them measured Kordos with her gaze.

"Shhhh!" The shepherd gestured with his fingers. "Why don't you come over and I will tell you!"

Only forty feet separated the two gardens' edges, yet this gap stretched more than 500 feet above the city.

"Are you mad?" Evert snarled.

Kordos answered not. Instead, he left the place swiftly. Minutes later, the crazy boy returned with a thick rope. Without a word, he cast it across the gap, and Niro caught it.

"Bind it to the balusters!" said the shepherd as he tied the other end to a post. Soon enough, a line stretched between the two castles, running spine-chillingly high above the earth.

"You daredevil…" Evert called out as Kordos climbed on the top rails, gripped the rope with his hands, and hooked his legs around it. They all gasped as the spider slid on the line, his back facing Norvita until he reached his friends.

"A crazy lad, indeed!" The prince shook his head and pulled him to them. Niro and Tashunko jumped on him, for they couldn't believe their eyes.

"How… Who… When…" were the only words to escape their bewildered tongues.

Kordos chuckled and hugged them both. "I promise to tell you everything."

Now his eyes fell on the maiden. "My name is Kordos!" he introduced himself.

The young woman turned red and stroked her hair.

"Edelin…" she said with a nervous smile, gazing at the handsome young man with striking eyes.

To his left, the young shepherd sensed Niro turning red, as though a sharp blade of jealousy was slicing through the boy's chest. Evert also seemed suddenly protective, and Kordos wondered if Edelin was his sister. If that was the case, then she must have been a princess…

That would explain why she looks so much like the queen…

"Well, Kordos, what's your story, then?" Evert placed his arm on his shoulder and ushered him to one of the cherry trees as all of them perched on the floor.

It was late morning when he began his tale, and two hours later, he concluded. He told them all about his escape from the Floating Islands, the flight on the dragon, and his visit to the hidden island in the North, skipping the cursed incident when he turned into a bloodsucker himself. It terrified him even now. Next, he spoke about the Cloak Castle, not mentioning Viggo, his dwarf friend.

"You should keep all this between us," he ended, with a serious note in his voice.

A silence full of wonder followed Kordos's story. At last, Niro started telling him all about the training with the Ghosts and the bet with Jeffry and his band. They roared with laughter when Tashunko described Lady Troll throwing them both to the lake.

But when Edelin recounted the two lads sneaking with tiny skirts to the Wilkens' backyard, all of them fell on their backs and held their stomachs.

Finally, when they composed themselves, she told Kordos that her father, King Wilfred was dying, which was why they all had come.

"The healers say he has but a few days to live!" she said with a choked voice. All of the merriment from moments before was gone, and she broke into tears.

Niro, who sat beside her, embraced her softly, and she sobbed on his shoulder.

Soon enough, all of them sank into a thick silence. They laid back on the soft carpet of white flowers and gazed at the drifting clouds. The sweet scent permeated the air, and a gentle sun caressed their faces.

"I must return to Cloak Castle!" Kordos stood up at once.

"I am coming with you," Niro said briskly. "It's time I paid a visit to Elmagos."

Tashunko bounced on his feet. "If he goes, so do I."

"Well..." Edelin eyed her brother, "it's kind of depressing to see Zigler every day here. I would much prefer to see Elmagos."

Evert was the only one who hesitated, but Kordos could tell that he had no power to change his headstrong sister's mind.

One by one they clambered on the rope, their young hearts booming like thunder. Even Kordos, the famous rock climber, quivered as a gust of wind shook the line.

They crossed the newly cleaned grounds while Kordos described how different it was only a day ago. There was no sign of the wizards or their busy gardening servants as they reached the Tree of Wands.

"Amazing!" Niro mumbled in awe as they all stared at the purple flowers falling softly on the ground.

"So the story is true," Evert whispered to Kordos, who nodded with a smile.

"I am starving!" Tashunko announced out of the blue, and they all smiled. The savage young man had an appetite of three men, but strangely enough, his body was muscular and athletic like a panther.

"There is food in Seros's room," said the shepherd.

They all followed him to the garden's doors, down the stairs, and through the hallway when loud voices echoed. The group froze, and the sounds from the dining chamber downstairs began to heat up.

"I say we should expose him for what he is!" Laos barked.

"We still don't have final proof," Petri answered. "Many of the Northern nobles support him. These accusations of the crown prince could drag us all into a bloody war."

"Any day we linger might cost us with blood!" Laos boomed.

"My friends!" Elmagos voice thundered, and silence fell. "We know for a fact he has deceived the rest of the regions, asking for coins that he used to build a secret Army and Navy. As we speak, his spies and followers are swarming the Northern Kingdom. If we don't act swiftly and decisively, a terrible war will be upon us, and Low Earth will be covered with fire and blood. I agree with Laos—Zigler must be exposed for the crimes he has committed and punished harshly!"

In the corridor above, the young group exchanged shocked glances. Finally, someone had the courage to bring the serpent prince to justice.

Kordos signed for them to follow him as he dashed down the curved staircase toward the table where the wizards sat.

The cloaks stared at them with open mouths. Before the green one could hurl lightning bolts from his eyes, Edelin hurried and gave him a loving hug. Niro and Tashunko trailed with hesitant steps, measuring Elmagos's eyes for a sign of welcome.

Laos and Petri muttered amongst themselves, wearing annoyed expressions at these young intruders.

"Is that what it has turned to? Children join us for a decisive and private meeting!" Laos snarled furiously.

"My friends," Elmagos calmed them down. "I trust these youngsters with my life."

The wizards' murmurs faded, yet their eyes scolded the group. However, when the emerald cloak gestured the four to follow him, he smiled no more, giving the shepherd a threatening stare.

He led the five of them back to the garden and reached the pavilion near the purple tree. There, Elmagos turned to Kordos, seized his shoulders with strong hands, and shook him violently.

"Did anyone see you? How did they come here?" The wizard's face reddened, and his green eyes were blazing like dragon fire.

Edelin's voice trembled. "No one noticed us, Elmagos!"

"We have been by ourselves in the Crown Garden all morning," Evert added, and the wizard loosened his grip. "No one saw us come over."

"I am sorry, my wizard," Kordos explained genuinely. "I happened to hear their voices and thought you would be happy to meet them."

Elmagos sighed. "I am glad you brought them here." He cooled as swiftly as he had blazed. "You must all keep in mind that Zigler's spies are everywhere. These are not ordinary days, and we all should be extremely cautious."

The youngsters turned serious and nodded.

At that moment, Tashunko's stomach grumbled, and all the grave faces, including the wizard himself, burst into laughter.

"Kordos!" Elmagos barked. "Your friend here is about to eat all of us alive. Why don't you bring some food?" He winked at the boy, who raced back into the castle.

While eating, the three Southern teammates told Elmagos all about their training, adventures, and the bet with Jeffry. The wizard's eyes twinkled with pride as he learned how much they had learned and acquired from their master trainers. But when Edelin shared the story of how they won the competition against Jeffry's team, he gasped.

"It was Niro who led us to victory!" Edelin's eyes glinted as she recalled Niro's wit and determination.

"It's true!" Tashunko said eagerly, a piece of bread still in his mouth. "You should've seen him. He was brilliant!"

Elmagos beamed at the boy with the golden mane and sapphire eyes. He nodded, full of pride.

"Like father, like son…" he mumbled and suddenly his face turned white. "With all that was happening, I almost forgot about my meeting with..." He paused, and then jumped to his feet. "Niro, let's go for a walk."

He led the boy outside, and once they were alone, he spoke with great joy.

"Your father is alive! I met him not a few days ago."

The boy froze like a statue, staring at the wizard's chest. "My father…alive?"

At once, he embraced the man with all the strength he had and wept tears on his cloak. Years of frustration, hopes, thoughts, and dreams condensed into that moment. His heart gushed like a river in springtime, overflowing its banks with raging water. For long moments, he sobbed and laughed, afraid of letting go.

At last, Niro calmed down. Elmagos shared with him briefly what Robin had told him that night.

"There was not a single day that your father didn't think about you. He loves you very much." With that said, the wizard smiled and put his arm on Niro's shoulder as they walked back to the pavilion.

Aromatic smoke enveloped the patio as the wizards puffed their pipes. Tashunko, Edelin, and her brother were sitting on the thick purple ground under the Tree of Wands.

"Over here, Niro!" the Black Tongue called, and Evert poked an elbow to his chest.

"Shhhhh... Someone might hear you from the Crown Garden!"

Niro came to them. His sapphire eyes were red from all the crying. Nonetheless, he stepped as light as a butterfly. A massive burden of uncertain fate and doubt had rolled off his shoulders, and his face glowed like the forthcoming sunset.

He sat quietly beside them and floated in his own world. The others exchanged strange glances, as though sensing that something significant had happened. They kept their mouths shut, giving him the space he needed.

On the patio, the shepherd made a small fire and boiled some water. "I will prepare you all an exceptional tea that none can compete with!" He added some herbs and a few dried leaves from a packet he carried.

The scent of cinnamon, clove, and ginger tempted their noses as Kordos walked to the wizards, pouring each a cup. Then he brought five more glasses to his friends under the tree.

"Remarkable!" Laos said with a note of admiration.

"Hmm…" Petri murmured. Outstanding…"

A pleased smile spread on Kordos's face as he handed them the tea. He was still standing when Niro told them briefly the news about his father.

"Are you Captain Quint's son?" Edelin asked with a shocked voice.

"I never believed the lies Zigler told about your father," Evert interrupted. "Although I was young, I remembered him as an honorable man and a loyal friend of the king!"

"This is great news and a blessed day indeed!" Kordos chirped.

Tashunko hugged his brother heartily and seemed as happy as Niro himself. Long years and many adventures these two had shared, and the bond between them was unbreakable.

"We should return to the Crown Garden!" Evert said to Edelin, and they all stood up. They departed from Kordos and promised to come back tomorrow.

At last, the shepherd sat down on the floral rug and rested his back against the trunk of the Tree of Wands. He gulped his tea and watched his friends shaking the wizards' hands.

The words about Niro's father gladdened his heart, and calmness fell on him. He closed his eyes, and the sounds around started to fade away.

Suddenly, hundreds of flowers sprinkled around. Kordos blinked. The boughs over him vibrated for a few seconds, then stopped.

When he looked at the patio, the wizards and the young group had frozen in place, gawking at the tree.

"Close your eyes…" A voice echoed in his head, and the boy obeyed at once.

An instant vision filled his mind. He saw a giant blue bird of prey, as large as a dragon, but with feathers. He had never seen one before. It was flying in wide circles in the midst of a thunderstorm. Lightning bolts struck its body and wings yet didn't seem to harm it. Nevertheless, the bird's yellow eyes transformed into light turquoise, the same color as the lightning.

Kordos opened his eyes just as a thin root crawled on his back and coiled down his right arm. A crack sounded. Next, the root swirled back to the ground. He picked the brown stick from his lap. It was about a foot long with a tiny turquoise hue at its tip. There were lines and indentations carved into the wood. A flat disc of silver, the size of a coin, sat at the base with a giant bird stamp on it.

Kordos stood up slowly and scanned the Tree of Wands, which appeared calm now as it dropped its purple blossoms. He plodded straight to Elmagos, his face as astonished as everybody else's.

At once, the pavilion buzzed like a beehive—the cloaks were talking over each other, while the young company peppered Kordos with questions that he could not answer.

"How?" Laos clasped the wand and studied it in disbelief.

"What did you dream about?" Petri asked with an interrogating voice.

"Did you hear a message?" Laos studied the boy as though he had something to hide.

"Silence!" Elmagos growled impatiently, and all turned quiet, even the birds in the trees. He glanced at the young group and asked each one of them to sit under the boughs of the Tree of Wands. One at a time.

Tashunko went, and nothing happened. Then came Evert, followed by Edelin and Niro. They did as Elmagos directed them, but nothing happened.

To the surprise of all, he asked Laos and Petri to alight under the tree, and again, no unusual motion appeared.

Finally, the green cloak sifted through the wand, studying the marks, the turquoise tip, the silver base.

"What was happening to me, Elmagos? What was it all about?" Kordos's voice trembled. After the cursed incident in Magisol, he hoped not to be in trouble again.

"Come with me!" The wizard gave him a swift glance and rushed back into the castle. He had no answer, either.

CHAPTER 14

THUNDERSTORM

Laos, Petri, and the young company marched behind Elmagos and Kordos, murmuring with anticipation. They had just witnessed something extraordinary and were quite mystified by it.

In the great hall, the three cloaks and the shepherd huddled around the dining table. Out of view yet in hearing distance, the youngsters were sitting on the bottom steps of the main staircase, ready to listen to a secret gathering.

"My friends!" Elmagos scanned the wizards' faces. "I am as puzzled as all of you, and I have no answer or explanation. However, none of us can deny what we have seen in the garden." He gazed at the baffled lad. "Kordos, tell us about your vision."

The boy could hardly stand. His legs turned heavy, and his heart was racing. *What the hell just happened to me*? He thought. But then, he cleared his throat and spoke with confidence.

"A giant blue bird of prey, larger than the eagles of Magisol, was flying in the midst of a thunderstorm. Its yellow eyes were fixed on me the whole time. Then, lightning bolts hit the creature but didn't harm it at all. When I looked at the bird's eyes again, they had changed to a shade of turquoise, the same color as the lightning. At that moment, I opened my eyes." Kordos ended, and utter silence fell on the chamber.

The wizards regarded him with different eyes now and darted no more suspicious or harsh glances. It was obvious they knew he spoke the truth.

"The marks on the wand are written in an ancient language which none of us are familiar with," Elmagos said.

"Perhaps we should consult with the folks on the Veerlands," said Laos. "They must know the meaning…"

"No! The only thing they would do is to cast him into the dungeons and throw away the key. Did you already forget what happened under the trees of Magisol?" muttered Elmagos.

Kordos shuddered in his chair.

"I am not certain," the green cloak spoke under his breath, "but I reckon Damaris gifted us a volume on this particular subject when she had visited us before the academy massacre…"

"There is one way to find out. Let's start at the grand library!" Petri proposed. "No worries, lad. When we find the book, we might have an answer to these marks and an explanation for your vision."

"What about the crown prince?" Laos asked.

"Zigler will wait!" Elmagos snapped and rose to his feet. "We must get to the bottom of it. My heart tells me there is something quite significant about his dream."

With that said, the three cloaks dashed down to the library.

At the table, the boy remained by himself, staring at the last wizard disappearing into the Neck. The sounds of rushing feet came as the four youngsters stormed at him.

"We heard everything you said!" Edelin gasped with excitement. "It is incredible."

"What does it mean, Kordos? Are you one of the wizards now?" the Black Tongue asked with an innocent note.

"Having a wand in your hand doesn't make you a cloak, my friend! We both saw what happened in Magisol," Niro said with a sarcastic tone. His words carried a hint of jealousy and bitterness.

"I am no wizard, Tashunko..." Kordos said quietly. "Niro is right. You need much more than a magic stick to be called one."

"Why don't we help them with their search?" Evert suggested.

"You wouldn't know what to look for," the shepherd answered. "They are searching for one particular book among thousands. Perhaps you should go back to Crown Castle. It might take them all night to find it." He looked weary and exhausted—the events of the day had taken their toll on his young mind.

"We don't need you to tell us what to do!" Niro snapped at him out of nowhere, and his face reddened. "We are here for Elmagos, not for you!"

Kordos, who had kept his cool until now, suddenly lost it. His jaw stiffened, and his olive-green eyes spat fire. At lightning speed, he shoved Niro with his strong hands and threw him to the floor.

"I am not here to take your place among your friends or Elmagos!" He stared at him from above. "I was happy to be a simple shepherd in the South. I didn't ask for any of this to happen. If you desire so much to be a wizard, take my wand; it's all yours!" He dropped it and left.

"He didn't mean to…" Evert tried to grab his arm, but Kordos raced up the staircase to Seros's room. His lungs felt aflame.

***

Niro sat on the floor, still dazed by Kordos's reaction. Though, in his heart, he knew he spoke the truth.

A firestorm of jealousy blinded his mind any time he had been around Kordos. Seeing Elmagos choosing the shepherd as his apprentice, and watching Edelin falling under his charm, cleaved him apart. But what most drove him mad was witnessing the Tree of Wands picking Kordos again while skipping him. That was too much for Niro's competitive spirit to swallow.

For the last nine years, he had followed Elmagos and learned all he could. Nothing spoke to him more than discovering his inner power and becoming a wizard one day.

When he stood, they all frowned at him. "I know! I know! I acted like a fool, and I am sorry!" he said with regret.

"It is not us you should apologize to," Edelin snapped. She seemed irritated and confused by her own feelings also. On the one hand, Niro knew she liked him, but on the other, everyone could sense she was thrilled by Kordos's presence.

"All right!" he said shortly. "I will talk to him when he comes down." They all seemed pleased and perched near the burning fireplace.

The evening turned to night, and the night crawled to dawn. Niro suddenly woke up and thought he heard some noises. On the other sofas, Edelin, Evert, and Tashunko were in a deep sleep.

The sounds came again, and the cloaks popped out of the Neck. They crossed the hall toward the drowsy band.

"We found no book or scroll about the marks..." said Elmagos with a weary voice.

The last day had been exhausting for the wizards. They restored the castle with magic, and then came the recent events and searching through thousands of books. At last, the tiredness caught up to them, as they began dozing one after the other.

Niro paced back and forth across the chamber. He recalled the details of Kordos's tale and dug deep into his razor-sharp mind for anything that he heard—or that Elmagos had mentioned—that might help.

Now, he whispered the words again. *Giant blue bird… Lightning…* He peeked through the windows. The sun was rising in the east.

A sudden shaft of light blinded him. Something in the room reflected it back to his face. Niro noted a broken mirror still hanging on the wall. He looked at his image and loathed himself for his foul behavior toward Kordos.

I turned into Jeffry…

Something came to his mind then. "A mirror…" His heart boomed. He now remembered that on their flight back from Magisol, the wizard had told him all about the vision in the mirror—how Primagos and the rest of the cloaks watched as the Three Widows stabbed the strangers…

"Elmagos!" he shouted ecstatically. Evert, Tashunko, and Edelin bounced as though someone had splashed them with a bucket of icy water. The wizards, who had been drowsing for just an hour, gave him an irked glare. Their red eyes were half-opened.

Niro stood beside the green cloak. "Perhaps there is a relation between Kordos's vision and what you saw in the mirror at Magisol. You had told me then that the Three Widows murdered two High Beings in the Cursed City, but rather than dying, one turned into a red-black flame and the other to a bolt of blue lightning."

Elmagos's eyes grew wide and glinted with golden fire. He jumped on his feet like a young boy and murmured Primagos's words:

"Now, for the first time since our order emerged, two more magical seeds are somewhere down there. Lightning and Flame. Each might establish its own order."

He kicked Laos and Petri, who had gone back to their dozing. "Didn't you pay attention to the clever lad? On your feet now!"

Elmagos put his arm on Niro's shoulder and went with him up the curved stairs.

"Brilliant you are! Absolutely brilliant!"

***

The door slammed to Seros's room, and poor Kordos leaped like a spooked cat. He was gaping with an open mouth at the stream of excited faces rushing through the door.

"Good morning!" Elmagos called as though they were all invited guests. The wizard, who caught Kordos's shocked face, gave Niro a nudge.

Niro sighed and approached Kordos with an apologetic face, yet the boy on the bed squinted his eyes suspiciously.

"Forgive me, my friend, I am really sorry." The sapphire-eyed boy smiled and handed him the wand. "I was a real fool last night and quite wrong to attack you."

The shepherd released his glare. "All is fine. It was a stormy day for both of us." As he grasped the wand from Niro's hand, an odd vibration crawled on his spine.

Niro took a moment to explain his realization, and moments later, Elmagos's voice thundered. "Now, when I recall the sights from the mirror in Magisol, I suspect our lad here received a glimpse of the new Lightning Seed."

He gazed at the boy. "Did you see any places in your dream? Mountains? Ocean? Forests, perhaps?"

Kordos shut his eyes and tried to revive it again, then he blinked and shook his head. "I am sorry, my wizard, there were only cloudy skies and the lightning storm."

"There must be something that we are missing…" snarled Elmagos.

"What about the Book of Magical Rainbow?" Niro pointed at the stand in the corner.

"What about it, boy?" Laos snapped with a defensive note. "This one is good for nothing. Seven drops of magical blood along with the Wolf's blood, is needed to open it."

"It was designed to create a new order on Low Earth, a colorful, magical rainbow of our own," Petri added. "Yet we never managed to have the blood."

A deep silence followed, but the green cloak pondered on something.

"Kordos, come here," said Elmagos as he moved toward the book.

"What are you doing?" Laos growled at his leader.

"This is not a game!" Petri barked.

"Do you have a better idea, eh?" Elmagos muttered. "Something extraordinary happened today, and we must try anything to get a clue. If not, we are all blind."

No one spoke. Hesitant, the shepherd walked to him. None breathed or made a sound. Then the wizard held the boy's palm over the rainbow grooves.

"No!" Kordos pulled it back, recalling what had happened in Magisol. Tears spilled on his cheeks.

Elmagos smiled softly. "Don't be afraid."

The boy sighed and put it back. Next, the wizard pricked it with his nail, and scarlet drops trickled on the seven grooves. As they touched them, they turned red, orange, yellow, green, blue, indigo, violet, black, and repeated the pattern. Kordos shut his eyes.

"Bloody hell!" Laos snarled. "Do you want to bring a cursed rainbow upon us?"

"It's on you, Elmagos!" called Petri.

The green cloak ignored them. "Evert, come here."

The Wolf prince obeyed like a soldier. Elmagos pricked his finger over the Wolf's head mark on the book. As the royal blood filled it, the head turned gray and the crown gold.

At that instant, bright white light dazzled the room as though the sun itself had been set in the ceiling. They all turned blind for a moment, covering their eyes with their hands.

Then, the intense glare vanished, and everyone blinked at the book. The grooves and the Wolf's mark were clean and empty of blood, and the cover was still closed. Kordos tried to open it in vain—it remained shut despite the dramatic spectacle.

"Is that all?" Niro asked with a disappointed voice.

Laos exchanged a glance with Petri and snorted. Frustration seemed to build on Elmagos's face as he muttered under his breath.

Suddenly, the shepherd noticed a parchment near his feet. At first, he thought it fell off Seros's desk, but when he picked it up, the paper glowed in his hands.

Elmagos snatched it. All gathered around him and gaped in wonder at the glowing sheet. In simple black writing, it said:

Beyond the endless green,

In the midst of a thunderstorm,

A lightning seed awaiting,

To stop a bloody war.

The thirstiest for blood must prevent

Low Earth from drowning in the red.

Elmagos slumped on Seros's chair. All stood in anxious silence, staring at their baffled leader. His lips moved without a sound while thoughts swirled through him.

Kordos had the impression that the wizard understood the meaning of these dark words yet had a hard time believing it was real. After long moments, he raised his green eyes from the paper and glanced at Kordos, who could not keep the fear from his face.

Elmagos's face hardened with determination as he rose up, tall and strong like a mountain.

"My friends!" he called with a clear voice, and all listened. "The last few days were full of revelations and surprises for us all. Low Earth appears quiet, yet underneath the calm surface, a terrible storm is brewing, waiting for the right moment to wreak havoc. The message on this paper is sharp and obvious!" He held it in the air. "I believe it's our last chance to save Low Earth. If we don't act swiftly, we might lose our only opportunity."

Petri's face turned tense. "What do you suggest, exactly?"

"I say we should prepare ourselves for a perilous journey!" Elmagos answered coldly.

"A journey?" Laos laughed nervously. "To where?"

"Beyond the Endless Forest! To find the Seed of Lightning."

"That's total madness!" Petri barked in annoyance. "No one has crossed the Endless Forest and come out alive! We don't even know if there is an end to that damned sea of trees."

"Elmagos," Laos added harshly, "there are many powerful creatures that we are not familiar with, yet you speak about it as if they are harmless woods. We are acquainted with just a small part of it, which is already crammed with Bloodsuckers and dangers like no other place. Have you forgotten how many Ghosts have paid with their lives? Who knows what lurks deep in the trees?"

"Both of you are right!" Elmagos insisted. "Indeed, the forest is dense and vast, and no one knows where it ends. Many good men we had lost there, and without a shadow of a doubt, it is full of perils. Yet not all of it is bad, and much is unknown. I believe most of the forest's dwellers do not seek to harm, and some might even aid us."

"Have you lost all reason?" Laos cried, all heated up. "Good creatures that might help us? When was the last time you encountered one? I know none!"

"I didn't say it would be an easy task!" Elmagos eyes flashed as he waved the paper. "This came to us from the Book of Magical Rainbow. It is a warning of what might happen if we sit here and do nothing. Time after time, the universe has presented us with signs and omens. I met Kordos at the Horns Game. Then we flew to Magisol, where he turned into a cursed one and still managed to escape. For the second time, I found him at Crescent Harbor in the most fortunate of an encounter. Then, he found the purple flowers in the Crown Garden, leading us here, to discover the Tree of Wands. In front of our eyes, it presented Kordos with a wand, and now the Book of Magical Rainbow gave us perhaps our final hint of warning. Should we close our eyes and turn our backs to all of these random events and signs? Or should we see them for the true omens that they are?"

Both wizards exchanged glances. At last, his words seemed to stir their hearts under their thick skin.

Kordos suddenly found his tongue.

"I will follow you wherever you lead, Elmagos, even to the darkest places of all!"

The green wizard twinkled with a nod.

"Well…" Petri muttered. "Our chances to survive are higher if we stick together. Besides, I had been craving a real adventure for some time now, so count me in."

"I am still uncertain about this venture…" mumbled Laos. "But you surely need my vast knowledge of plants and animals."

"Where Elmagos goes, I am with him!" Niro called swiftly and dashed beside the wizard.

The Black Tongue stepped beside his friend. "I will bring much shame upon my tribe if I don't join."

Before Edelin and Evert offered themselves to be part of the risky journey, Elmagos interrupted.

"We shall go, but the four of us only. I would not risk another soul!" His voice was firm as he put his hands on Niro's and Tashunko's shoulders.

"You are my eyes and ears!" he whispered to the two Eagles and the two royal siblings, all four of whom seemed deeply hurt by his decision. He smiled at them all to comfort them. "There are only a few I can trust, and you are among them. Remember! This quest of ours must be kept secret. If our enemies discover our purpose, they will stop us any way they can!"

"When do we start?" asked Petri.

"By the end of the Wizards' Game, after we settle our account with Zigler. If we leave now, it will create too much suspicion."

All nodded in agreement.

"At least we shall enjoy some delicious food and wine before passing through hell," Laos muttered.

Gongggg… Gongggg… Gongggg…

The gigantic bell in the Crown Castle shook the peaceful morning. The puzzled faces in Seros's room trembled with each deafening chime. At once, all rushed to the balcony while numerous distant bells joined the orchestra, ringing throughout Norvita.

Edelin glanced at Evert with a ghost-white face. They bolted out of the room, raced across the Cloak Garden, and climbed the rope back to their castle. Niro and Tashunko followed them, for they knew something bad had happened.

"Elmagos, what is it?" Kordos asked as he noticed the wizard's grave face staring ahead.

"King Wilfred Lukos is dead!" he replied sadly, "and at the worst timing of all."

CHAPTER 15

MOURNING AND HOPE

Around the dining table, Kordos and the three cloaks were eating a plain breakfast. None had talked or made a comment. Each was busy with his own thoughts.

The wizards were cherished friends with the Northern King for many years, until the cursed day when his elder son died. After that, the lively Gray Wolf was never the same. He became bitter and distrustful even of his oldest companions.

Suddenly, Elmagos stood up and raised his cup. "To our friend, Wilfred! May his strong spirit join his honorable ancestors, the Gray Wolves of the north."

A shiver ran through Kordos's spine as they all cheered. Now, the cloaks began to share pleasant memories. These were the early days of the king when he was vigorous and full of wit and laughter.

Breakfast had passed, and the boy headed to the garden, sitting on the patio bench all by himself. The morning sun caressed his face yet gave him no comfort at all. A swarm of fears and doubts stormed at his young mind and stung relentlessly like furious wasps.

Kordos glared at the purple tree with blaming eyes. *You gave the wand to the wrong person,* he thought. *I am just a simple shepherd, surrounded by mighty wizards who fought glorious battles and led Low Earth with their wisdom.*

Nonetheless, the Tree of Wands continued to drop its endless flowers, disregarding the boy's concerns.

Now, I am a member of a perilous quest. How can I contribute and not be a burden? What if one of the wizards dies? It is my journey, after all. Why should any of them risk his life to get the seed?

The voice tortured his mind and planted fright and guilt in his heart. Kordos was so troubled that he missed the sounds of steps until someone stood behind him.

"Cast aside your troubles and fears!" Elmagos smiled and sat beside him. "We all volunteered for this journey."

"What if someone dies on my quest? I would never forgive myself!"

"My lad…" The wizard scanned his pale face. "You do understand what is on the line here, don't you?"

Kordos reflected for a few moments. "I do, Elmagos."

"It is your vision we are after, yet the journey belongs to us all. This quest is full of dangers and challenges even we wizards have never faced. None of us could do it alone!"

The bronze color came back to Kordos's face, for the words soothed him.

"We must not fail!" Elmagos said with an icy voice and gazed at the purple tree. "We have to find the Lightning Seed at all costs, for I fear it's our last hope to stand against the next dark storm. Too many threats from all directions are drawing near to Low Earth. And now we are as divided as can be, forgetting that we share the same land, culture, and history. But the ones that concern me the most are the Fangs. Our heroic Ghosts are doing a miraculous job, yet they are barely enough to hold back the wave of carnage. Once the Three Widows attack with their full force, their army will flood Low Earth with waves of blood. The parchment only confirmed my greatest fear:

A lightning seed awaiting.

To stop a bloody war.

The thirstiest for blood must prevent

Low Earth from drowning in the red.

Now you understand why we can't take the risk and send you alone. Your failure might be the doom of all. Together, we have a better chance to succeed."

Kordos's voice trembled. "What use can I bring to a group of great wizards, if not being a burden…"

"Nothing…and everything!" The green cloak winked at him. "But if you plan to doubt yourself on each step of the way, you had better stay here, for you will become useless trouble indeed."

The boy lowered his head, but Elmagos continued.

"But if you bring the victorious spirit and certainty I witnessed on the Mother Bear cliff; we should all be grateful that you join us. Sooner or later you must decide if you want to get back to the shepherd's life or discover the wizard within you. The Tree of Wands had already made its decision...now it's your turn. Nothing great will happen without your consent."

"Thank you for your wisdom and guidance, Elmagos." He smiled at him with admiring eyes.

The wizard walked out of the pavilion when he suddenly turned back, remembering why he came in the first place.

"Ahhhh, my lad, I almost forgot," he said. "Before we go on our risky adventure, I must send you on a short one."

Kordos opened his ears like a donkey.

"Later today, Laos, Petri, and I will attend the King's funeral ceremony, and the following days of mourning require our presence at many events. I need you to ride toward Crescent Harbor. When you reach the main road along the bay, find Romi's Inn and don't leave until Captain Quint arrives!"

"Niro's father?" Kordos asked with a baffled tone. "Don't you prefer to send his own son instead?"

"No, Niro should stay here," said the green cloak decisively. "The Wizards' Game is only a few days ahead, and the team should prepare themselves."

"What should I do when he gets there?"

"Tell him everything that has happened here in the Cloak Castle, and don't skip a thing. Then you shall bring him to the opening ceremony in the Northern Arena to watch his son."

The boy's mouth fell open while a broad grin spread on Elmagos's face.

"But Cap—" Kordos found his tongue, but the wizard cut him short.

"I know. Robin Quint is the most wanted man in the kingdoms, you say, and they will catch him and sentence him to death!"

"That's right!"

"Now that King Wilfred has died, so too must the unjust judgment of the captain, for it was all based on Zigler's lies. It's about time to fix a terrible injustice and clear Robin's name forever."

"But Zigler is the lawful heir. He will never accept it!"

"On my dead body will he be crowned King of the North!" Elmagos's eyes blazed. "According to the laws of Low Earth, the Wolf King must be confirmed by the Den of Wolves and the guardians themselves. Without our approval and blessings, none shall sit on the Wolf's throne. Instead, Zigler will be exposed for his crimes and plots, and he will be judged by the new rightful King of the North, Evert. He will offer a full pardon for Captain Quint and his men and restore their honor!" Elmagos ended with a smile.

"When is all of this supposed to happen?" Kordos sounded anxious.

"After the six days of mourning, which happens to be the day of the opening ceremony of the Wizards' Game. There, in front of tens of thousands of people, justice will prevail."

Moments later, the two went to Seros's room, where Kordos packed quickly. Once he was packed, Elmagos handed the boy his wand.

"This is yours. Keep it safe until you learn to use it."

They left the room, but as he was walking down the hallway, Kordos recalled Seros's advanced teaching books.

"I forgot my coat..." he said and turned back to the room. At once, he dashed to the shelf, picked up some of the magical study books, and stuffed them into his bag.

I will have much idle time at Romi's place, he thought.

With his leather coat on his shoulders, he left the room and hurried in the corridor to reach the wizard.

They came down the stairs and passed through the library and many chambers. Kordos couldn't believe his eyes. The castle looked fresh and clean now, and much of it seemed in neat condition.

At last, they arrived at the underground passage. "Don't let anyone see you," Elmagos said, "and be wary on the road."

"Thank you for everything, my wizard." The boy embraced him strongly. "It is an honor to accompany you. I won't let you down, I promise!"

The green cloak gave him a smiling nod and closed the hidden door.

Down the old stairs Kordos went, and through the old tunnel he marched, until he entered the crypt. He sneaked out like a thief and got a horse from a stable.

Grieving faces wandered the streets of Norvita, and not a sound of laughter could be heard. The Northern people loved their king, and his painful death left them orphans. Uncertainty captured many now, for none knew what was about to come.

The boy spurred his mare toward the west, and as he galloped through the gate, he dropped the unease behind the city walls. Farms and groves dotted the Fork Valley, and the wind blew on his face. Some fresh air was all that he needed.

He followed Elmagos's advice and took the main road along the Lukos River. It was broad and well-paved, and now and then he passed riders and carts with horses traveling to Norvita.

News of the king's death must have reached the shoreline, he thought, for the people's faces appeared grave and gloomy. Sometime later, he approached the boundary of the Fork Valley. West of it, a vast pine forest stretched all the way to Crescent Harbor.

For long hours, Kordos rode through pines and cedars. His sharp eyes found curious hares and squirrels hiding behind trees and ferns. On some occasions, he even spotted black bears and deer. At last, the river and the road curved toward the north, and when it turned back westward, a sudden gust of salty wind welcomed his face.

He could taste the sea on his tongue as the infinite blue blanket unfolded before his eyes. An hour before sunset, Kordos finally arrived at Romi's place.

The harbor's main road seemed half empty. He tied his horse in the back and walked through the tables to a wooden counter, where a maiden stood tall behind it. Her golden hair glinted as though under the sinking rays of the sun, and her blue eyes twinkled.

"I need to speak with Romi, please. Is he around?"

"I am Lena, his daughter, and you are?"

"My name is Kordos. I am here on behalf of Elmagos the Green," he whispered.

Her eyes kindled at once, and a deep voice called from his left.

"Come over here, lad!"

Kordos strode toward a hefty man, soaring six and a half feet tall and carrying a girth that had swallowed many casks of ale. His round face was masked with gray hair as he measured the youngster with a doubtful glance.

"Are you Romi?" Kordos asked.

The big man nodded. "Where is the old man hiding?"

"I came by myself. Elmagos stayed behind with the others," he whispered. "He sent me to deliver a message for a particular sailor…"

The man's blue eyes opened. "That seaman was supposed to be back here already, according to my count. You can wait for him here. Meanwhile, Lena will show you a room."

But when he caught his daughter's spirited face beaming at the newcomer, he pulled Kordos to him.

"Actually, let me take you over there myself." He smiled tensely while she gave him an unhappy snort.

***

All day long, the Crown Castle was hectic with preparations. People were rushing through the chambers, arranging all the necessary matters for the Wolf King's funeral.

Some hours before sunset, the gloomy procession had begun. The Royal guards carried Wilfred's coffin through the main street of Norvita. Queen Enya, Edelin, and Evert, with Zigler and his son Osmond beside them, were walking behind the casket. All were dressed in crow-black clothes. Behind them marched the three wizards, garbed in ashen cloaks rather than their typical colorful ones. And last strode the ministers and counselors, lords and leaders of the Army, giving the last seed of the Gray Wolf a well-deserving departure to the afterlife. On both sides of the endless file, the people crowded and grieved for their beloved king as the coffin passed by them.

Every ten seconds or so, thousands of horns howled like a host of wolves, a final cry from the broken pack to their leader. Edelin shuddered in grief each time, and more tears flowed on her cheeks.

And so it was that when the red ball of fire was diving into the Sapphire Sea, Wilfred Lukos, the descendant of the Gray Wolf dynasty, was buried in the Ivory Rock. There, he joined all his legendary forefathers in peace.

It was a dark day for the Northern people, full of grief and sorrow. But when all returned to their homes, the sadness turned into fear and despair of an unforeseeable future.

The coming days were incredibly difficult for Edelin, Evert, and the queen, realizing that King Wilfred was no more. They spent their time mostly by themselves, wandering through the Crown Garden. Neither Enya nor her children seemed interested in what the future might bring.

Niro and Tashunko, who had been staying at the arena with the other contestants in the last few days, visited Edelin and Evert a few times. Any time her teammates came, she felt light again and set aside her sorrow. By now, the princess realized how deep their bond and friendship grew, blessing the day she had joined the Southern Team.

The boys were not the only ones to visit the royal family. Elmagos kept coming daily. He dug into the depths of his skull and told them tales about Wilfred the man, before he became a husband and a father.

On the fourth day of mourning, he met them for an afternoon tea in the Crown Garden pavilion. The trees and plants bloomed and permeated the air with fragrance. Elmagos scanned the queen's face. Her eyes were much less red and swollen than the days before, and her bright smile spread on her face more frequently.

Edelin and Evert also seemed in a much better mood, and the wizard sensed the time had come to discuss the future.

"Enya..." he said softly, as a father speaks to his precious daughter. "I know you are still mourning your husband, and I wish I could wait a bit longer, but I can't. We must talk about what lies ahead."

She nodded with an understanding smile.

That morning, Elmagos told her all about what had happened to him since the day he and Kordos left the Crown Garden. Enya seemed in utter shock. The stories about the Cloak Castle, the Tree of Wands, the investigation, and the meeting with Robin Quint overwhelmed her. She gave her children shocked glares, for they knew most of what had occurred while she was kept in the dark.

"Everything happened so fast, and then Father died," Evert said with an apologetic tone.

"We were about to tell you, Mother..." Edelin grabbed the queen's arm and rubbed it with her face.

Elmagos continued his astonishing story, telling her all about Kordos and the wand, the Book of Magical Rainbow, and the warning parchment that came from it. Finally, he concluded with their decision to begin the quest for the Lightning Seed.

"How is it possible?" She mumbled with awe. "Is this young man supposed to be a wizard?"

"We are all as puzzled as you…" He shrugged. "But no one can dismiss what had occurred in front of our eyes, nor what we discovered."

"Oh, Mother!" Edelin called with sparkling eyes. "Watching him under the Tree of Wands was breathtaking."

Enya glanced at her daughter's face. "I knew she would like him, didn't I, Elmagos?" She said, all pleased with her motherly intuition as the princess blushed like a ripe tomato.

Then came the moment of truth. The wizard unfolded his plan regarding Zigler and the Northern Kingdom. At last, he said, "Evert, I have been watching you since you came to this earth as a baby. I believe with all my heart that you will be a great king, just and honest with all. You have your father's strength and mother's insight, and you will need all of them to mend the evil Zigler has done. I have no doubt you will restore the honor of the Northern Kingdom."

He measured the young man as his mother and sister hugged him warmly. The prince, who seemed uncertain at first, gazed back with his gray wolf eyes at the man he cherished like his own father. His chiseled face turned hard and determined as a rock.

"I accept your trust in me, Elmagos," said Evert with a clear voice, and he bowed slightly. "I pledge to bring back our lost dignity, once again, to the first days of my father."

Queen Enya kissed him on the cheeks, and tears of joy trickled down her delicate face. Her wounded heart seemed to have a moment of peace while she was still mourning her beloved husband.

They all left the Crown Garden with a smile on their faces, for the future contained a gleam of hope.

***

On the fifth day since the king's passing, Elmagos entered the Royal Hall but saw none except the cook. The short man hurried through the chamber, carrying a tray with food and wine.

"Where is the queen?" He asked.

"She is in her room, not feeling well, and asked to be disturbed by no one!" he spoke with an annoyed voice.

Elmagos cared not and trailed him to her chamber. The cook knocked on the door, and it opened seconds later.

In the hallway, the wizard lurked and stood by the open door. Enya looked at him with red, swollen eyes. Her tan face had turned pale as cotton.

"I told him that you asked not to be bothered, my queen!" the cook said with an irritated voice as he stepped out. Elmagos gave him a blazing glance, and the man scurried back to the kitchen in terror.

"What is it, Enya?" He asked softly, and she burst into a hysterical cry. He embraced her warmly, and she cried for long minutes on his chest until no more tears came.

"I had a terrible night…" She gave him a regretful smile. "I finally realized Wilfred has left me all by myself."

"You are not alone, my dear. Many people love and care about you." His eyes twinkled at her. "I will take my leave now…go to rest."

He was about to shut the door when he heard the queen's voice.

"Elmagos, please come with the wizards tomorrow night. We shall have the last mourning dinner for the king's memory," Enya said with her back to him.

"Of course we will come. Feel better, my child." He closed the door, but as he walked in the hallway, a strange sensation crept into his heart. He headed to Edelin's and Evert's rooms, yet no answer came when he knocked.

Perhaps they are in the garden, he thought. And so he returned to the Cloak Castle and pondered many things, including Kordos and Robin.

***

Five days swept fast as the shepherd waited at Romi's place, helping the big man with many tasks around the inn. But most important of all, he was around Lena.

The two watched sunsets together and shared many laughs. Anytime she turned up, his young heart boomed with excitement. For the first time in his life, the youngster fell in love.

The captain hadn't arrived yet, and Kordos hoped that Robin would come on the sixth day of mourning.

That would give me another day with Lena before we leave for the Wizards' Game, he thought.

Like each night since he came to the inn, the boy sneaked to the back yard, making sure no one was on his tracks. Then he slid into the well, climbed down the ladder, and pushed himself through the secret door. Yet, that night his heart stopped at once. Candlelight flickered from the underground room. At last, he was about to meet Captain Quint.

When Kordos opened the door, Robin stared at him, all puzzled. He didn't know the boy's face and seemed to expect Elmagos or Romi.

"Who are you, boy?" he asked with a suspicious voice.

"My name is Kordos, Captain! The wizard sent me here to deliver you a message." He caught Robin's face under the dim light, which seemed quite disappointed.

"Very well," he said indifferently. "But before I can digest anything you say, my stomach must have something to eat, for I am hungry as a wolf."

"Certainly, sir! I will bring you something from the kitchen and inform Romi you are here. He was quite concerned about you," Kordos added and left the room.

Less than five minutes passed before Romi and the boy popped up with baskets of food and bright smiles.

"My good Captain!" the innkeeper beamed at Robin and gave him a bear hug. "I thought something bad happened."

"Nothing to worry about, my friend, just a short delay," he said quietly. "Many ships were sailing toward Crescent Harbor, so we had to be extremely careful."

"Ahhh... Yes...of course!" Romi smiled. "The Wizards' Game starts two days from now. My friends who dwell inland told me the Northern Kingdom is packed with visitors from all regions, and all the inns are fully occupied."

"Or it might be for the king's mourning week," Kordos suggested indifferently. "On my way here, I saw many mourners traveling toward Norvita."

Robin's face turned white. He slumped on the chair as though he bore a massive boulder on his back.

"King Wilfred...is dead?" His voice trembled, and his eyes sank with sadness. "When?"

"Five days ago." Romi sighed and smacked Kordos's head, who felt he deserved that and more for his insensibility. Now he sensed how much Robin loved his old friend, despite all that happened in the past.

They set the food on the table, but the starving captain seemed to lose his appetite. "I would do anything to speak with you again, my brother…" Kordos heard him mumbling with saddened eyes.

"Well, my boy," the innkeeper snapped impatiently. "Now that our man is here, you can finally tell us what Elmagos sent you for. The lad refused to tell me anything until you came; can you believe that?" Romi smiled at Robin.

At once, Kordos started telling them all about the Cloak Castle, the Tree of Wands, and the Book of Magical Rainbow. The boy didn't miss a thing, following Elmagos's directions.

Then, Quint heard about the wizard's plan to crown Evert as the new King of the North and bring Zigler to justice. Finally, he and his men would retain their lost honor, and he would unite with his son.

"Elmagos reserved you a seat beside the rest of the wizards, so you can see Niro better than anyone else."

Kordos beamed at the captain and watched Robin's eyes sparkling like diamonds. Tears trickled on his beard, but he didn't try to hide them. Long moments he sat and smiled like a toddler who has no troubles on his mind.

"When shall we head to the arena, my young wizard?" Robin asked respectfully.

"The ceremony starts on the day after tomorrow in the late morning. If we get on our way some hours before dawn, we should arrive on time."

"To Niro and the Southern Team!" Romi toasted, and they all cheered and sipped the wine.

***

That night and the day after crawled in Robin's mind, who yearned to see his son. However, to Kordos, the time flew by like a dragon's flight, for he cherished each moment with Lena. His lovely maiden seemed extremely confused by her father's behavior since Robin's arrival. Romi, who used to watch their steps like a hawk, now seemed to encourage the young doves to spend their time together before the boy left.

Kordos wanted to tell her all about the secret quest and everything that had happened to him in the Cloak Castle, yet he had to be secretive, just as Elmagos had made him promise.

"Do you love me, Kordos?" She asked softly while they were gazing at the setting sun on a lone rock high above the harbor.

"I do, Lena! As I love the Thousand Knolls with all their scents and blossoms," he whispered in the maiden's ear and kissed her lips. That evening, under the sparkling stars of the Northern sky, she kept warm in his arms.

Hours before dawn, the innkeeper woke Kordos and the captain. They all sat around a loaded table as Lena and Romi's wife served them hot tea and fresh-baked bread. Both thanked Romi and his family for their hospitality, and the girl kissed the lad on his lips. The proud parents exchanged a smile and accompanied their guests outside.

In the courtyard, Romi handed Robin a gray robe with a hood. "Cover your face until your name is cleared, my friend."

"What would we do without you, my brother?"

The captain hugged the big man, and off the two went on their way.

CHAPTER 16

A RISKY PLAN

The night of celebration was finally over, but for Half-Lip and Dabi, tough days of gruesome practice followed. Nevertheless, the two brothers began to accept their roles and trained with the utmost intensity. Both realized that if it weren't for Neal fighting beside them, none of them would have survived the arena. They realized that they needed to sharpen their skills quickly if they were going to survive.

It was another sweaty morning in the courtyard when Lord Marlo Eckhart approached Gorgos, holding a piece of paper in his hands.

"Warriors!" Marlo called. The sounds of clashing swords and shields stopped at once, and all glanced at him with puzzled eyes. "Tomorrow, there will be a glorious celebration in the arena, where our leader himself will honor us with his presence. Our four victorious warriors will be given the high honor of executing the enemies of Low Earth!"

Then Lord Eckhart spoke in Gorgos's ear and left the drilling ground with a broad smile.

"Neal, Pozzo, Half-Lip, and Dabi, step forward!" the master trainer called. "Our lord has commanded me to take you all to the arena so we can practice the ceremony to perfection. It is a rare privilege, so you'd all better take it seriously."

An hour later, they passed through the arena's main gate, and memories of the skirmish seized Half-Lip's mind.

"Master Gorgos, what should we expect, exactly?" he asked as he walked behind him.

"An execution!" he snapped. But when all of them stared at him with calves' eyes, he sighed impatiently and explained. "People who committed treason, or went against the leader's orders, are sentenced to death by the executioners. The crowd usually picks the most beloved fighters from the arena, which tomorrow will be the four of you. It seems that you made quite an impression in your first performance."

Gorgos continued with a note of resentment in his voice. "But to be honest, it is not so much of an execution as it is a slaughter. The traitors are pushed into the ring with no weapons while the warriors are fully armed. I believe you don't need my tactics for this kind of fight."

No one asked any other questions. They all seemed even more horrified than their first battle—and disgusted with the idea of slaughtering innocent people.

They drilled the ceremony routine many times until Gorgos seemed content. On their way back, he ushered them through the underground part of the arena. Half-Lip stared in anguish as they passed by the cells where the people were kept before their fight.

The vivid memory of the agony and unbearable anticipation grew in his mind. He recalled how his heart exploded with each of the crowd's cheers. A sensation of nausea went through his chest and up into his throat. He was about to vomit when voices sounded from behind the bars.

These were the traitors Gorgos had mentioned, and none except Half-Lip dared to look inside as they hurried down the dim corridor.

"Half-Lip! Move forward!" the trainer barked as he caught him staring into the cell. Nonetheless, the boy froze like a statue, his legs refusing to answer. He was gaping in disbelief and horror at the faces of the enemy.

Alec and Lia stared back at him.

"Half-Lip!" Gorgos bellowed and whipped in the air. His voice echoed and shook the walls. The scared lad bolted forward and left his fellow Eagles behind.

"Do not test my patience, boy!" the baldheaded man snarled in his face as they headed back to the fortress.

***

At lunch, Neal, Pozzo, and the two brothers were sitting at a table.

"What did you see?" the Eel asked Half-Lip under his breath. He had been watching the boy for the entire meal, and he could tell that something wasn't right.

Half-Lip's face turned white and depressed as a graveyard. "Alec and Lia were locked up with the traitors. Tomorrow we are going to execute my best friends!"

Dabi dropped his food on the plate, and his eyes screamed with horror.

"How is it possible…" Neal muttered and shook his head. "They were on the *Skulls Cleaver* when we left."

"No…no…no…" Pozzo muttered with a painful expression.

"How many others were in the dungeon?" Neal asked after a long silence.

"Fifteen people, more or less," Half-Lip murmured as he recalled the desperate eyes and hopeless faces behind the bars. "We must help them!"

Dabi nodded at once.

"We all want to do that, but how?" Pozzo said with a genuine voice, yet none could answer.

Neal's sharp mind swirled with thoughts and ideas, but nothing seemed workable.

Suddenly, he noticed Rusty at the far wall, guarding the entrance to the warriors' cells. He needed to send him a message, but how? Then an idea popped into his head. He raised his hand and signed Cler to bring some water.

As she poured water into the glasses, Neal whispered with a swift tongue.

"Tell Rusty to meet me at the warriors' latrine!" She stared at him fearfully, but she approached the red-haired guard and gave him a cup of water, passing the message along with it. Then she rushed back to her duties.

A minute later, a figure sneaked out to the warriors' latrine.

"Neal…" a voice rustled.

"Right here!"

There wasn't a moment to waste, so the Eel told Rusty what had happened that morning, and about Alec and Lia in the cell. Rusty's face turned pale, and he scratched his head in agitation.

"They chose us to be the executioners of these prisoners!" Neal hit the wooden door with a furious fist. A cruel vision of poor little foxy butchered on the sand haunted him now. "We must find a way to save them, Rusty, or else we all die in the arena."

Neal's harsh words struck a chord. Something had to be done, no matter the risk.

After lunch, Neal complained about a sharp pain in his knee, and Gorgos became quite nervous. The pirate was their biggest asset, and Lord Eckhart instructed him to keep him in good health at all times.

"Come with me!" Gorgos ordered and led him to the healer's room. When they came in, the healer was all by himself, arranging the herbs and medicine jars.

"Hello, master trainer." He smiled at him and peeked at the other face. "Ohhhh, look who is here…our most famous warrior." The old man winked at Neal.

"You must check his leg!" Gorgos snapped impatiently. "Make him ready for the execution tomorrow, or our lord will be furious!"

The threat in the trainer's voice sparked a fire under the healer's feet. He bolted to the Eel and ushered him to one of the beds.

"They think I am a wizard! Fix his ankle…mend his arm…" he grumbled as Gorgos left the room. At once, he pressed around the kneecap, spread some sort of a brown paste, and bandaged the warrior's leg.

"Your skills are on par with a wizard, master healer," Neal said, giving him an admiring gaze.

The man snorted. "To them, I am no better than a slave."

Neal noted the bitterness in the healer's words. The time of the silver tongue had come.

"A slave?" He uttered in disbelief. "Talent such as yours should be cherished and appreciated everywhere. Many are the men who hurt and kill, but rare are the ones to heal." He gave a slight bow, and both men smiled.

Soon enough, they found themselves speaking about all sorts of things when Neal asked indifferently, "How does a master like yourself find himself here, on this bloody island?"

The old eyes studied the warrior's face for a long moment as though debating if he should trust this stranger.

"Well…" he sighed. "I was a healer in the Royal Army for many years until one day they released me from service. I didn't know what to do, or where to go. I had to feed my family in the North, yet no one wanted to hire an old man.

"One day, a loyal friend told me about an opportunity to earn a good deal of money. In my great desperation, I begged him to introduce me to these people. Soon after, I found myself here, on this island, and under the command of Lord Eckhart. At least I earn some coins now." He gave a sad sigh.

Next, Neal told him some adventures from his past—excluding many details, of course—and the healer could hardly believe his ears. As they shared more stories, the old man became fonder of the fascinating pirate. He had not one friend in the fortress.

"I had some problem sleeping the last few nights," the Eel said with a troubled voice. "Do you happen to have something that might help?"

The healer gave him a self-important smile. "I prepared an herbal powder for the lord for the same reason. But it's a costly one!"

Neal gazed at him with craving eyes, and the old man seemed to enjoy each moment.

"Mmmm…well…I guess on some special occasions, I might break the rules!" His eyes sparkled like a mischievous boy, and the Eel patted his shoulder warmly.

"I can't thank you enough, master!"

The healer walked to one of the shelves and picked up a green jar. Neal's eyes tracked him like a hawk as he took a tiny amount with a spoon and wrapped it with paper.

"There you go." He handed him the precious powder. "This should hold you for a week! Be careful to put just a bit. If you take more, you will sleep like a bear in the winter, and even death couldn't wake you up!"

"You are a true mate. I will use it precisely as you suggested, not more, and not less." The silver tongue spoke while his crafty mind was cooking a scheme.

***

A few hours later, Cler slammed the healing room door in a panic.

"Master!" she gasped. "One of the guards fell on his back. He is on the steps outside and in much pain!"

The healer bolted toward the stairs, where he found Rusty moaning in pain. The maiden gave Neal a bright smile as he dashed to the jar and filled a bowl with the green powder.

"What are they cooking for dinner?" He asked.

"Meat and vegetable stew."

"Good!" He handed her the powder and whispered his plan. "You must do as I tell you!" he insisted as she stared at him with wide-open eyes.

He smiled at her.

"Don't worry, maiden. You will be just fine."

She nodded with a tense smile, grabbed the bowl, and rushed out of the room. On her way down, Rusty winked at her while the puzzled healer tried to find the problem with his back. Moments later, he forced himself up, still moaning.

"I think it's slightly better. But perhaps I should lay for a short time in the healing room." He groaned and supported himself on the poor old man.

***

At last, nightfall came. The warriors finished their final meal of the day and were escorted to their cells, just as they were every night. Then the guards and all the people that dwelled in the fortress gathered for dinner in the formal dining chamber. All attended that night and toasted the exceptional honor Lord Eckhart would receive in the arena.

Cler followed Neal's directions and mixed the powder secretly into the food and wine. Neal had told her it would take about half an hour before all of them would fall asleep in their chairs. But he was wrong.

Cler was so nervous that she spilled large amounts of the sleep-inducing herbs, and soon the men were dropping and squashing their faces on the tables.

Meanwhile, one friendly Bloody Shirt was speeding through the dark, passing from one guard to another, handing them cups of wine.

"A toast for our lord!" He smiled at each and didn't leave until they drained their cup.

Soon enough, the only people left standing were Rusty, Neal, and Cler.

Rusty took the keys from the guards, hurried through the corridors, and opened the slaves' and warriors' cells. "Remain in your place and don't make a sound!" he ordered, and no one dared to talk or move.

Moments later, he led a long file to the courtyard, where all the captives gathered.

In the meantime, Neal, who had disarmed the snoring guards of their swords and bows, gave these weapons to the warriors.

"We are going to escape this shithole!" Rusty said with a quiet voice. "You will follow Neal's commands without questions, or all of us will die tonight!" He scanned their faces, and all nodded obediently. They already trusted the Red Angel with their lives.

Next, Pozzo brought out Bloody Shirt uniforms and handed them to the warriors. "Wear it as they do!"

There were more than sixty of them, and about 150 slaves—a large number to hide.

At last, they got out of the fortress. Ten figures garbed in the cursed red uniforms mounted horses and scouted ahead. The rest marched on foot. Rusty smiled at the dark, moonless sky as he led the long column into the forest.

They crowded among the pine trees and sat in utter silence while the leaders discussed the plan.

"Rusty!" Neal said shortly. "We should ride to the arena at once and free the prisoners. Four of us would be enough to handle the few guards."

The seasoned Sea Ghost warrior seemed troubled as he studied the doubtful faces around him. "We must be swift and stealthy with our attack!"

"No, Neal, one mistake and all is lost. It's only you and me this time!" He gave the pirate a meaningful stare. He trusted none other for the mission.

"Half-Lip, Dabi, Pozzo!" the Eel spoke to the three. "Guide the people through the trees and toward the east until you see the harbor lights. Wait for us there."

"If we don't come back in three hours," Rusty added, "do as your heart tells you."

With that said, the two men prepared their weapons, jumped on their horses, and vanished into the night.

They galloped across the valley until the sight of a huge shadow loomed ahead—the arena. They ushered their beasts into a nearby apple grove and hid them there. At once, they rushed through the trees and knelt at its boundary, spying at the arena's gate.

Three guards were huddled around a small fire near the gate. Rusty clasped his bow and drew an arrow, but Neal seized his arm.

"No..." he whispered. "If we miss, the others will cry for help. We must do it from close!"

"Alright," the red-haired pirate nodded. "We do it your way!"

Moments later, they stood and strode like two regular guards toward the men at the gate.

The three sentinels were laughing hysterically and seemed a bit drunk. Neal and Rusty stepped closer.

"Hey, what are you doing here so early?" one called, and his friends laughed. The two newcomers said nothing, only waved their hands. About ten feet from the group, the Eel and the Sea Ghost flung their knives and pierced two of the guards' chests.

The last one standing reached for his sword, but he was late. Rusty sprinted and leaped forward, slashing his throat. Nonetheless, the bastard managed to give a faint cry.

Cold sweat covered both their faces. Fortunately, no footsteps or voices sounded, and the two exchanged a relieved glance.

Neal searched the corpses, grabbed a bundle of keys, and hastened to the gate. It opened with a slight sound, and they crept downstairs into the dim corridor, which led to the underground cells. Suddenly, a peal of laughter echoed.

The Eel ducked behind a corner and gritted his teeth. Two guards were sitting on wooden boxes, playing cards and blocking their way to the prisoners' dungeon.

Both warriors drew their bows. "Three…two…one," Rusty counted, and two arrows cut through the musty air and pierced the men's throats.

Sounds of rushing steps came from within the cell. Stunned faces crowded behind the bars and stared in disbelief at the two Bloody Shirts approaching with their weapons ready.

"Neal…" a girl's voice whimpered.

"Rusty!" a boy whispered.

Lia and Alec were gaping at them with wide-open eyes. Rusty unlocked the iron door and scanned the frightened shadows as the two Eagles jumped on their saviors, refusing to let go.

"Follow us…we cannot linger!" Neal ordered and dashed through the corridor, leading all of them in silence.

Minutes later, they passed through the arena's gate and ran to the grove. Neal lifted the helpless captives on the two horses and urged the rest to run behind them.

"Time is against us...push forward!" Rusty was grabbing the ones who plodded wearily at the back.

An hour after, they reached the forest and hurried eastward through the trees. Suddenly, two shadows ran at them, scanning the new faces in the dark.

"Alec!" Half-Lip called, embracing his friend while his mute brother hugged Lia. At last, the three young members of the Nestless Eagles came together once again. However, time was pressing, and they couldn't delay another second.

"Neal!" Rusty uttered with urgency. "Let's go to the front. We must find a way to capture a ship." The reunited group followed their steps.

Both men and the youngsters crept through the cedars for long minutes. Then they halted and lay on the ground. The harbor with its many docked ships sprawled beneath them. Bloody Shirts were patrolling with their lanterns all around the docks and the main path.

"There are guards next to every ship!" Neal growled with frustration.

"There are too many of us to sneak around!" Half-Lip mumbled, and the rest agreed with him. Precious minutes passed, and their faces became tense and doubtful.

"I think I found a way…" the Eel said with a smile on his face. His eyes glinted as he unfolded his idea.

Next, Neal, Pozzo, Lia, and the three lads gathered the slaves and warriors and explained what to do. The armed men grouped behind the Eel and southward marched under the cover of the trees. They lurked near the southern part of the harbor, about a hundred yards from where the first ship was docked.

Neal crawled forward and surveyed the dock. It was the least-guarded section, protected only by a few guards.

Meanwhile, Rusty was riding north through the trees parallel to the shoreline. At last, he noticed the northern-most pier. He tied his horse to a tree and descended the slope. Like a wild cat, he stepped with graceful balance and stealth until he hid in a bush, thirty feet from the waterline.

Fortunately, the four guards patrolling the main harbor road had their backs to him. He crossed the road with speed and disappeared behind a rowboat. Moments later, he ran low down the pier and climbed aboard the last ship. Rusty took one of the lanterns, poured some oil on the boards, and placed the flame on it. The fire blazed on the surface, spreading quickly to the masts and sails.

Loud screams came from the dock as he caught many lights racing toward the burning vessel. Soon, blowing horns sounded, and many more guards were speeding from the southern piers to lend aid.

Rusty crept down the back of the blazing ship and slid into the freezing water. He swam to another one while the Bloody Shirts were filling their buckets with water, trying to put out the flames.

When he reached the next ship, he climbed aboard, slipped through an opening, and dashed below deck, where he started another fire near the mast. Finally, he climbed out of the window and swam back to the dock.

It took long minutes for the baffled guards to notice the smoke coming from the second vessel. Terror and confusion grasped them all as they were running and screaming in chaos.

With a sly smile on his face, Rusty came out of the frigid water, crossed the path unnoticed, and sprinted back to the forest.

***

When Neal saw the great fire blazing to the north and all the guards leaving their positions, heading toward the fire, he gave the signal. A long column of figures marched through the shadowy trees, down the long pier, and to the first ship. In less than five minutes, all the liberated slaves and warriors were on board.

"All sailors, step forward!" Neal spoke with a calm voice, and dozens gathered around him. Most of them were pirates—some he knew. Alec and Lia also joined, after the novice training they had received on the *Skulls Cleaver*.

At once, Captain Eel assigned the seamen to their posts, and the ship turned into a beehive. Men were rushing on the deck, climbing on the masts, unfurling sails, and tying ropes. In a few short moments, the ship started pushing through the water and away from the pier.

"Still no sign of Rusty!" Alec called nervously.

"He will come!" Neal smiled with confidence, yet he darted a concerned glance to the dock.

"Lia, go to the captain's cabin. There must be a map that shows the course through the Treacherous Sea. Bring it to me! Without it, we are all blind and in grave danger."

A minute later, Alec and Lia dashed back with a parchment. Neal snatched and opened it beside a lantern. A pleased smile curled on his face as he studied the map. "Excellent job, foxy…"

"Look!" a man's voice called beside the captain, pointing down the pier. A Bloody Shirt was speeding toward them, and a hundred yards behind him, a pack of guards with torches was running and screaming. It was clear by now that they had noticed the moving ship.

"It's Rusty!" the Eel chortled to Half-Lip, who stood beside him.

"Neal!" the Sea Ghost howled from the dock, gasping for breath as he ran. "You are a genius!"

The legendary first mate of the *Skulls Cleaver* was ready to jump into the water when two arrows flew toward him from Neal's ship.

"Nooooo! You fools!" Captain Eel screamed as he charged like a raging bull at the warriors on guard, knocking them down to the deck. They were certain Rusty was one of the guards. When Neal raised his steaming head, Rusty was lying motionless on his back with an arrow skewering his chest.

The Bloody Shirts arrived shortly after and surrounded the body as they glared with vengeance at the escaping ship.

"The Red Angel is dead..."

Some of the slaves sobbed as the word spread around, and Neal let out a wail of anguish. Boiling tears trickled down his face. He slammed and kicked things around him as he marched like a madman, terrifying all on board. For the first time that night, many eyes seemed to question if this famous captain would deliver them out of the Treacherous Sea—or sink them all into the icy depths.

CHAPTER 17

THE ARENA

The morning was crisp and bright, and about two hours before midday, Kordos and Robin approached the Fork Valley. The boy watched how a sheen of excitement ran on the hooded man's face as they crossed the lands he had almost forgotten.

When the Northern arena came to sight, both gasped. Behind the two towering castles, the enormous oval-shaped structure was the third most impressive wonder in the North. It was so immense that it could hold 50,000 people inside. Built of gray stones, it seemed as though a gigantic raincloud had landed in the midst of the grassy ground.

Thousands of people were traveling along the roads and dressed in all sorts of fashions and colors, each according to his custom. The two blended in the crowd, and none paid any attention to the youngster and the old man.

When they reached one of the gates, Kordos pulled out two stamped papers Elmagos had given him and handed them to the sentinel.

"The Wizards' honorary section..." The guard's eyes opened with awe. "It's right there; follow me." He pointed to a red balcony, raised above all seats.

"Who are you?" The man asked suspiciously as they walked among the multitude.

"I am Elmagos's apprentice, and this is my father. The wizard invited us to be his personal guests, as you see in these tickets!" the boy said shortly, and the guard nodded with respect.

All of this time, the lad held Robin's arm. He had a scarf wrapped around his face and was acting like an old man.

At last, they reached the Cloak Balcony, but to their utter surprise, none of the wizards were there.

"Perhaps they are giving their teams a final pep talk..." Kordos shrugged. He scanned the arena and couldn't find an empty seat. "So many people…" he murmured with awe.

"About 50,000, to be exact." Robin shifted uneasily on his comfortable cushion, nervous and exhilarated.

"Wait here, old man!" Kordos laughed. "I am going to wish the Southern Team good luck and tell your son to look for you here."

"This will be an exceptional day…" The captain slid the scarf away from his face, exposing a broad grin.

The boy chuckled and hastened through the crowd. People gave him annoyed stares, but he cared not. All he could think of was Niro's face when he would see his father up there on the balcony.

Loud horns blew all around the arena, and Kordos stopped in his tracks. He was just above the front rows overlooking the arena's battleground. The crowd's applause shook the place as the teams entered one after the other, waving their colorful flags.

Then, an entourage accompanied by the Royal Guards passed through the main gate. They headed toward a scarlet stage that was set at the center of the battleground. Sentinels in golden armor and white cloaks held the Gray

Wolf banners, and Zigler and the high council took their seats on the platform.

Kordos stared in disbelief. He felt as though someone had stuffed an apple in his throat, and no air could pass.

Where are the wizards? Where are Evert and the queen? The panic took him as the horns sounded again.

The arena went silent as an old man stood up. He was the head of the royal council.

"My lords and ladies, people of the North and Low Earth. I am here to present the only rightful heir of the Northern Kingdom, the eldest son of our beloved King Wilfred, Zigler!"

Everyone rose to their feet, cheering and clapping.

A cold sweat covered Kordos's body. Nothing made sense to him. He peeked at the Cloak Balcony and saw Robin's face turning white under the hood.

Zigler stood and thanked the councilor. Then he addressed the crowd.

"My brothers and sisters of the North, lords and ladies, honorable guests and people of all regions, welcome. Seven days ago, I lost my father, and you lost a great king. He was a ruler who understood the hearts of the common people and the minds of the nobles. On his deathbed, he named me as his successor and swore me to be a strong king and a shield of the Northern people!"

The crowd stood on their feet again and applauded eagerly for long moments.

"Last night, I dined with our dear wizards and the queen. It was the last memorial dinner for my father, and we cherished his memory with tears and laughter. Before they retired, the guardians of Low Earth gave me their blessings and decided to crown me today at the opening ceremony. But this morning, when we tried to wake them up, they lay dead in their beds!" Zigler called with fury, and 50,000 hearts stopped.

The murmurs and sobs and cries spread through the people like fire in a field of thorns. Agony and grief grasped the multitude. Soldiers carried three coffins into the battleground and placed them on the sand in front of the platform. Green, blue, and orange fabrics masked them.

Kordos fell on his knees and wept. At the corner of his eye, he saw Niro and Tashunko falling on their faces and crawling toward the caskets.

The damn horns blew again, and the thousands gazed back at the stage.

"After losing our leader and king," Zigler cried with a booming voice, "and praying the bad days are behind us, came this despicable evil, the assassination of our beloved heroes. My guards discovered that the wizards had been poisoned by the Crown Castle's new cook. It was an unknown poison, and a deadly one. When we caught him hiding in the city, the wicked killer confessed his crime. Then he gave us the name of the man who sent him to commit the murder!"

The arena turned into a graveyard, and a thick tension that could be cut with a knife spread through the seats.

"The man who had murdered my brother Owain nine years ago is the same man that was behind this horrible evil. At this moment, he is mocking our terrible pain from the Cloak Balcony, trying again to take the North to himself. The vile murderer Captain Quint!" Zigler screamed hatefully as he pointed to the balcony.

Now all eyes were gazing at the single man standing on the balcony. Vengeance burned his flesh as the serpent prince tricked him again.

"Zigler!" Robin thundered and removed his hood. "You loathsome bastard! You plotted against me to seize more power for yourself, and now you killed the wizards when they didn't support your claim!" the captain shouted with rage, and the crowd began to murmur. "People of Low Earth! All my life I served you in the Navy with honor, and never cared for prestige or wealth. Now I swear by all that I hold dear that I speak the truth. This man is no Gray Wolf, but a venomous serpent and a shame to the honorable Lukos dynasty. Not only that, but he is a filthy murderer, and he will spread fire and hatred, war and blood everywhere! And if you don't stop him now, he will carry his viciousness to all regions!"

"Seize the traitor!" Zigler screamed with panic, and soldiers rushed toward the balcony.

Niro, who had stared at his father the whole time, couldn't believe his eyes. Now Zigler's men were beating and dragging the captain through the seats. A fire of rage blazed through Niro's bones and boiled the blood in his body. He bolted like a tiger from his cage, raced across the sand, and knocked down two guards on his way to the platform.

Niro jumped on Zigler like a frenzied animal and punched his face with a fierce fist. Before he could land another blow, he sensed a sharp ache in his back. Someone knocked him on the neck from behind, and the rest restrained him.

Just as the guards helped the bleeding Zigler rise from the floor, the second tiger attacked. The mighty Tashunko stormed the ring of men around his brother, beating one after the other with speed and strength. Five collapsed to the ground before someone hit him on the head.

The crowd fussed, and many people booed, questioning Zigler's honesty. At once, he rose to his feet with blood on his face and boomed in a commanding tone.

"Open the gate!"

The spectators fell in silence as hundreds of fully armed Bloody Shirts marched into the arena and surrounded the platform.

"If any traitor has something to say to your king, speak now!" he shrieked like a pig.

Suddenly, a Bloody Shirt blew a horn. A heartbeat later, thousands of horns answered from the outside, shaking the walls and the hearts of everyone inside. None dared to say a word, and a tense hush fell on the arena.

Zigler motioned to the old councilman. "We shall begin the crowning ceremony!"

After taking an oath like the kings before him, Zigler sat on his father's chair as supporters cheered with excitement, yet others seemed less enthusiastic.

Then came the Royal Army and Navy commanders, who swore loyalty to the new King of the North. Behind them strode the Northern lords, who each bowed before Zigler. At last, he stood with the crown on his head, and the crowd applauded.

"Now that our dear guardians are gone from this world, our enemies will test our strength and try to attack us at once. None can protect us except ourselves. To be strong, we must be unified under one banner and one king. Low Earth won't survive under scattered banners—it must become one united kingdom again. Under my rule, we will be powerful again, and conquer new lands loaded with treasures and gold. Soon enough, we shall take what is ours, by will and by force! Tens of thousands of Bloody Shirts, my loyal army, will fight on your behalf!"

The crowd erupted in applause again.

Kordos scanned the thrilled faces in disbelief. *These fools already forgot the captain's warning and the wizards' deaths,* he thought. The snake on the stage had mesmerized them all.

His heart darkened with hate and vengeance as he glared at Zigler. The boy was about to burst into the battleground and avenge the wizards when he caught a glimpse of Niro and Tashunko on the sand, beaten and humiliated.

His eyes wandered to the three coffins, and tears flowed like rivers. Then it dawned on him that all the cloaks were gone from Low Earth, and he was the only one left, a young wizard who barely knew how to use a wand.

Think, Kordos…think! I must help my friends and Robin, but how?

"My people!" Zigler called again. "We came here to celebrate the Wizards' Game, yet it must be canceled now, for the guardians are no more!"

The crowd grew restless, and many booed and muttered. The new king raised his hands, and the murmurs stopped at once.

"Instead, I am proud to bring back the ancient tradition of our kingdom. So old, it almost has been forgotten. As your king, I present to you the Blood Games!"

A grave silence followed his words. Then, some murmured with excitement while others grumbled in resentment. These were brutal contests of armed men fighting to the death, and it didn't appeal to all.

"We should all cherish and worship the mighty warriors and accept their sacrifice. Shall we begin?" Zigler cried, and some of the cheering spectators seemed more zealous than before.

The Bloody Shirts dispersed to the perimeter as the Royal Guards left the arena, accompanying the king and his high council to the Crown Balcony while servants dismantled the ceremony stage.

Kordos dashed through the front seats and found himself twenty feet above Tashunko and Niro. They were both bound.

"Niro..." Kordos whispered, and the lad opened a sapphire eye. His gloomy face was covered with sweat and sand. Then he elbowed the Black Tongue and motioned for him to look up.

"My friends!" Kordos muttered swiftly. "You must stay alive, no matter what. I will find a way to help you!"

At once, he vanished into the multitudes as a few of the guards headed to the boys.

Horns sounded, and all gazed at Zigler, who stood proudly in the Crown Balcony.

"What should be more fitting for a murderer and traitor such as Captain Quint than to watch his only son fight for his life in the arena? Bring forth the boy and his barbarian slave!" he called, and thousands of spectators began shouting.

Three men dragged Robin to the perimeter wall that surrounded the battleground and forced him to watch. Beneath them, the Bloody Shirts gave Niro and Tashunko light chest armor, a helmet, and weapons of their choice. Both boys took two swords each and prayed Marc and Ganix trained them well enough to survive.

"As these two savages attacked my men earlier, I ask now for two volunteers!" Zigler commanded. All of his personal guards stepped forward with fire and vengeance in their eyes.

"Excellent!" The king measured them with a broad grin. "A difficult choice, for all of you are fine soldiers.

Sevrin and Baro, you are chosen!" Zigler chuckled as though he had chosen two of his finest warriors.

One took a spear and a sword, while the other a sword and a shield. Moments later, they faced Niro and Tashunko in the center of the arena.

"Are you ready to die, boys?" Sevrin, a hefty man with an ugly face, chortled as he spun the spear shaft swiftly in his hand. The Black Tongue growled at him like a mad dog, his black eyes piercing the two men.

"Let the Blood Games begin! For death and glory!" Zigler thundered, and the people cheered feverishly.

Clashes of swords and war cries rose as Tashunko fought Sevrin and Niro battled Baro, slashing and blocking, shoving and kicking.

The spectators gasped with surprise, mesmerized by the young warriors who fought like lions.

Three minutes into the fight, Niro blocked Baro's sword and slashed his thigh. The man screamed in pain and fury while the boy seemed startled by the spraying blood. That split second where he lost his guard and focus cost Niro dearly. His wounded opponent thrust his shield into the boy's helmet and knocked him to the ground.

Niro's head whirled. He opened his eyes to find his enemy snorting like a pig above him.

Each moment seemed like an eternity as Baro had the point of his sword ready to skewer the lad's chest. Tears blurred his sapphire eyes, and the man turned into a misty shadow. The thousands held their breath, but Robin gave a cry that shook the arena.

"Nirooooo!"

The captain's scream quivered Tashunko's bones, who was in the middle of a fierce attack against Sevrin. The Black Tongue gave a swift glance to his right as Baro lifted his blade to pierce his brother's heart.

With lightning speed, he flung a sword at Niro's foe, and it pierced his thick neck. The man dropped dead on the lad.

Niro shoved the bleeding corpse to the side and jumped to his feet as the crowd screamed madly.

At that moment, Sevrin thrust his spear at Tashunko, who dodged left and curved his abdomen like a bow. The spearhead stung only the air, and Tashunko gripped the shaft with his left hand and cut his enemy's arm with his sword. The severed limb dropped to the ground.

Sevrin fell on his knees and wailed in pain, staring at the Black Tongue with terrified eyes.

The young savage removed his helmet and cast it on the sand. His long black hair scattered on his face. His black eyes pierced the shaking warrior more than a sharp blade.

"You volunteered to kill and spill blood, ah?" Tashunko growled at him and, with a swift blow, decapitated him.

The arena fell silent. No one uttered a sound as the stunned faces stared at each other, not knowing how to react.

The Black Tongue lifted Sevrin's head high in the air and glared at the frozen crowd.

"Is that what you came for? To see blood?" he shouted hatefully and hurled his enemy's head into the first rows. It fell near two noble ladies in the front seats, who fainted at once.

"Tashunko! Tashunko! Tashunko! Tashunko! Tashunko! Tashunko!" Fifty thousand people were screaming and beating their hands wildly. They had turned mad.

Both lads froze on the shaking ground, flabbergasted and gaping at the frantic fans with disbelief. Suddenly, a fat, bald man crossed the arena and stood between them.

"The victorious warriors of the first Blood Game battle! Tashunko and Niro!" He raised the boys' hands up.

Niro's eyes wandered to the Crown Balcony. The crowned serpent rose to his feet as he scanned the screaming faces. It was obvious that he didn't expect this outcome. Nothing could calm the zealous crowd until the horns blew again.

"Take them to the dungeons beneath the arena, where the other prisoners are kept!" Zigler ordered his guards, and they rushed toward the boys.

Tashunko clasped his sword tight, refusing to let go.

"Don't give them a reason to kill you now!" Niro said. "Drop it to the ground, brother. Today, no one will recall that they crowned a king, but they will surely remember your performance. For now, it is the only revenge we have left." He spoke with a cold voice, and Tashunko released his blade as the soldiers approached.

***

Kordos had tears in his eyes. His friends were alive and survived this hell for another day. Now he had to use his wits and find a way to save them. He watched the guards as they pulled the two boys through one of the side gates and down a stone staircase.

A few minutes later, they appeared again, dragging two men in chains up the stairs, and locked the iron door behind them.

So this is where they keep the prisoners, thought Kordos as the horns sounded. The bald man marched on the sand again.

"These two traitors who served in the Royal Army refused to obey the orders of their new superiors. Therefore, they will fight to the death!" the man called with a dramatic voice. Soon after, the terrified men chose their weapons, and the match began.

Swords and shields clashed and banged but failed to impress. A minute into the battle, it seemed that they didn't want to hurt each other. The onlookers lost their patience and started booing. Next, the master of the game gave an agitated signal, and a dozen arrows flew at the two fighters, piercing them from all directions.

Then, Kordos saw a group of Bloody Shirts hauling Captain Quint out of the arena. The captain had been badly beaten and could barely stand.

Kordos raced through the seats and followed from behind.

"Swhere are you faking him?" a guard rasped. He was ugly as hell, and there were less than six teeth left in his mouth.

"By the king's order, this dog is taken to the Navy Fortress prison!" answered the man who held Robin's arm. "They have there all the necessary means to make him talk, if you know what I mean." He winked, and his friends laughed viciously.

"Ton't vey plan to hang him tsoday?" The ugly guard smiled as he sprayed spit all over their faces.

"No they tson't!" A tall Bloody Shirt mocked the toothless man and shoved him aside. "Tsey vill hang him on the last zday of the games, two zdays from now."

"Curse you, ithiots!" he screamed as the laughing guards approached the main gate, dragging the captain with them.

Kordos followed them from behind and lowered his head, trying to avoid any looks.

"You there!" a harsh voice called from his left, and the boy froze in his spot. He was a few yards from the gate.

A heavy hand grabbed his shoulder, and his heart boomed like the battle drums.

"Don't you enjoy the show, boy? Is it too harsh for your delicate soul?" A sentinel taunted him with a sweet lady voice, and the rest snorted like boars.

"Leave the boy alone..." said his friend, and Kordos stepped forward, not looking behind him.

Die, you swine! Kordos was trembling with rage as he hurried through people and searched for Robin.

Suddenly, he noticed the captured captain and a long Bloody Shirts file, all mounted on horses, heading west. They galloped away, leaving clouds of dust and despair.

Kordos slumped under a tree just outside the arena and wept. His strength was melting away, and a shadow darkened his mind. He was desperate and had no idea what to do—or where to start. The wizards were dead, and a vicious king had been crowned. In the bloody arena, his friends were prisoners, and death hung over their heads every moment. Captain Quint was captured and about to be tortured in the Navy prison until his execution.

Where are Evert and Edelin? The boy asked himself.

He needed help, and the only place that came to mind was the Crown Castle. Perhaps he would find Queen Enya and her children there.

Loud voices came from the arena's main gate as guards were carrying long boxes and loading them on a wagon.

The wizards! thought Kordos and dashed toward the cart. An old man was arranging the coffins so they all fit on the wagon. Two women were sobbing quietly as they laid flowers on them.

"Ahhh…" the old man sighed sadly. "Many people I have laid to rest in my life—lords, nobles, even a king. But never did I imagine burying a wizard, no less three of them! A sad day, a cursed day…" He peeked up as gray clouds covered the sun and it began drizzling. "The sky is crying for their beloved sons. It's time for me to move."

Suddenly, he noticed a lad as he pushed the heavy coffins tight next to each other. Kordos tried not to look inside the coffins, but he failed. Now he saw the pale, lifeless faces of the guardians. His eyes swept on Laos and Petri with agony, but when they found Elmagos, he burst in tears. All the memories he had experienced with the wizard flooded him now, threatening to drown his young spirit to the ocean floor. He couldn't breathe as he craned over the mighty green cloak trickling on the dead face. *Rest in peace, great one…*

"Give me a rope!" Kordos spoke with a choked voice. The old man handed him one, scanning the youngster as he tied the boxes together.

"Now they won't slide," he explained as he gazed at the stunned old man.

"Thank you, my boy!" He nodded with a pleased face. Then he moved to his seat.

"Where are you taking them, sir?"

"To the Castle District in Norvita. I need to prepare the corpses for the funeral."

The man slapped the reins. The horses neighed, and Kordos stared at the wagon rushing toward the east.

Without thinking, he raced beside the old man, who watched him all puzzled and halted the steeds at once.

"I knew one of the wizards very well. Let me be with him," the boy said sincerely as he bent down and caught his breath.

"Alright, then. Climb up, my lad!"

Kordos climbed aboard in silence. Rather than fleeing away from danger, the young shepherd was about to return to the most treacherous Den of Wolves.

ABOUT THE AUTHOR

G.H. Babagilo is a traveler and lover of life. He has traveled widely and lived in many countries throughout Europe, Asia, Latin America and the United States.

His interests and activities are broad and diverse ranging from flying airplanes, backpacking, rock climbing and dancing the Tango.

His writing comes from the depths of his soul and the heights of his imagination.

G.H. Babagilo loves to hear from you, so please feel free to visit www.babagilo.com to join the email list, receive free giveaways, get the latest exclusive news, connect on Facebook and Twitter, and stay in touch!

Made in the USA
Las Vegas, NV
23 June 2023

73783041R00173